An Inspiring Butterfly Anthology

KALEIDOSCOPIC QUILL

Edited by

Demi Michelle Schwartz
& Andie Smith

CONTENTS

INTRODUCTION

Dear Butterflies,

Welcome to the kaleidoscope!

Thank you for soaring into the butterfly anthology of my heart and soul. At this moment, you're fluttering on the precipice of a literary metamorphosis, a colorful adventure penned by the special authors and poets whose pieces await on these pages. Each and every one of them picked up their quill and brought their unique hue to this collection, and you're in for a magical journey.

But before you fly into the stories and poems that promise to guide you in your own transformation, I want to back up and share how *Kaleidoscopic Quill* came to be.

This book started as a seed of an idea, a newborn caterpillar. At the time, I had no way of knowing what Kaleidoscopic Quill would become, but that's the beauty of metamorphosis, isn't it? You embrace the unknown, then emerge from your cocoon, spread your wings, and discover all you were destined to be. This anthology underwent that same transformation.

It's no secret that I love anthologies a little too much, so naturally, I wanted to lead one of my own. The obvious choice for the theme was butterflies.

For as long as I can remember, I have loved butterflies and all they symbolize, especially hope and freedom. These beautiful winged wonders remind me to search for the light in the darkness, the color when everything is gray, and the sky when gravity is dragging me down to the ground.

Once I started my journey as a songwriter, butterflies quickly became part of my brand, and people in the music industry began associating me with them. I was even wearing a butterfly dress when I won my first music award.

But then, I got more involved in the publishing industry, and I realized that butterflies weren't just a symbol of mine as a songwriter, but a symbol of me as a person. So, I decided to bring my love for butterflies into the publishing world through an anthology.

I have a very clear memory of being on a call with Abigail Wild, the owner of Wild Ink Publishing, trying to gain the courage to ask her if I could lead my own anthology. Instead of directly asking her, I decided to be hypothetical. Did my casual snooping session for info go as planned? Nope. The conversation went something like this.

Me: "So, how does someone get to have an anthology through Wild Ink?"

There was a short pause.

Abby: "Do you want to lead one?"

Yeah, I was that obvious.

I told her about my idea for a butterfly anthology, and she asked me to send her a pitch for the project. So, as soon as we got off the call, I wrote the pitch, sent it to a friend for feedback, then emailed it to Abby and tried not to panic. It wasn't long before Abby told me the project was on the publication schedule.

I was like, what?

And just like that, *Kaleidoscopic Quill* was in the works.

After the project got approved, I had to choose my editor, my butterfly partner in crime, you could say. There wasn't even a decision. I knew I wanted to work on this book with my fabulous friend, Andie Smith. To my absolute delight, she agreed to be the lead editor, and the butterfly court was born.

As the anthology's announcement approached, I started to get worried. What if no one wanted to write for a butterfly anthology? What if no one in the writing community loved butterflies as much as me?

I shouldn't have panicked, though. The response that the project received on announcement day was beyond my wildest dreams, and as soon as the submission window opened, stories and poems began soaring into my inbox. Reading the pieces and seeing others' share what butterflies mean to them made me realize that this anthology would be something very special. The pieces in this book aren't just creative works about butterflies. They're precious gifts, glimpses into their creators' hearts.

Within these pages, you will find yourself immersed into poems and stories that explore a kaleidoscope of butterfly symbolism—hope, freedom, love, transformation, spirituality, peace, and beyond. When you finish reading, I hope you're a different person from who you were when you flipped over the cover. I'm definitely a different person from spending so much time with these wonderful pieces, from the submission period to the editing phase. The contributors exceeded my expectations and dreams for this anthology in every way, and because of their creativity and vulnerability, *Kaleidoscopic Quill* will always be one of the most special books in my life.

To Abby, thank you for allowing me to publish this anthology through Wild Ink and for being part of my journey in the publishing industry. I have learned so much from you over the past couple years, and for that, I'm so grateful.

To Andie, thank you for being the best butterfly sister in the universe and for working on this book with me. I love you to the kaleidoscopic moon and back.

To the authors and poets, thank you for trusting Andie and me with your words and your hearts. It has been a true honor watching your pieces undergo their own transformations and earn their wings.

And to you, dear reader, thank you for picking up *Kaleidoscopic Quill* and for embarking on this inspiring journey of metamorphosis. The sky is the limit, and I wish for you to flutter your wings and soar with purpose, hope, and joy.

With love from your Anthologist and Butterfly Queen,

Demi Michelle Schwartz

1

WHO WILL I BE?

BY DANA GRICKEN

The future is unwritten
A blank page in a history book
But I wish I could peek ahead
And take a quick look.
Who will I be
What will I become?
What will I do?
Will I help anyone?
Will people think of me
After my life is done?
So many possibilities
And things I can become.
The adventure
Has only just begun.
Like a flower in bloom
Like a butterfly out of my cocoon
Metamorphosis, here I come.
But it is still a mystery
Of who I will be
And what I will become.

2

UNCOCOONED

BY MICHELLE SANCHEZ

The light rouses me. Slow to rise, filling my enclosure with a warm, pink glow as a cacophony of loud caws break the entombing silence. I shiver at the sound, every instinct warning me to hide.

I stretch my limbs oh so slowly, needing to remind myself of their tender ache. My body has lengthened, and it's difficult to move now. I have outgrown this dwelling.

This silken cocoon is all I can remember, and cold fear ripples through me as my stomach quakes with an unfamiliar hunger. Will this small space be both my beginning and my end?

No... I refuse to believe it.

Hope has seeded deep inside me. A small voice that insists there must be more to my existence than this.

I'd rather live a short life in that warm light than die safe within these walls.

I trace my fingertips along the thin silk streaked with veins that glitter and glisten.

Am I ready? Is it time?

My limbs have become stronger with each rise, and

something deep within me whispers, “Yes, you are ready, daughter. Spread your wings and fly.”

I place my palms on the thin barrier, applying a pressure I never dared to before. As I watch breathlessly, my beautiful prison falls to my feet in silken threads.

I am...

Unhindered.

Uncrowded.

Uncocooned.

Unencumbered, my vision floods with a myriad of colors. A deep blue embraces the light that now glows so bright I can’t look at it directly. Lush green growth sways before me, moved by the same cool breeze that caresses my cheeks and dries the tears of my rebirth.

This is it. There’s no returning to what once was.

With such wonder before me, I wouldn’t resurrect my cocoon even if I could.

In a swift motion, I extend my limbs to rise powerfully behind me.

I am strong.

I am beautiful.

I am brave.

Leaping into the air, I finally taste the freedom of my first flight.

And then...

With a surge of my strong and silken wings,

I fly toward the light.

3

MIGRATION | TRANSFORMATION

BY REBECCA MINELGA

Alone she flutters; alights on a petal; drinks deep. She is unbound, untethered, unhindered. She dances on the breeze, no fear of falling. Pale light energizes cold muscles, thrilling her hemolymph. She is a voyager, an adventurer, a free spirit.

Alone, she crosses the stage, accepting the first accolades of adulthood. She runs, she flies, she tastes the goodness of the world, she crashes, she soars again, always stronger. She is enough. Always pushing, always striving, always rising.

Chill nights and multi-hued days, the slow transition from green to gold. A cooling sun is slower to bring life each new morning. She chases it, but lazy basking days are gone. The air nips her wingtips, now chasing her.

She falls again and does not rouse. Her broken wings run with wax, feathers falling, burned and blazing. Alone she flew, alone she fails. Friends, family, old flames long forgotten. The ambition she's chased is a tiger's tail. If she lets go, she is lost.

Her wingbeats slow. The last fading rays dapple through sage leaves shot through with brilliant clusters of orange, night-deep black. She wavers, drifts, falls, recovers. She climbs, each labored flutter nearly her last.

Shattered, her spirit sleeps, existential exhaustion dragging her deep. Days pass in the daily grind, bone-weary, burned out, barely surviving. Nights lengthen, slumber her only respite.

She waits...

Are you okay?
Let's get coffee.
I've been there, too.

Dawn breaks, and she is not alone.

Paper bark and the scent-taste of honey, citrus, pine. A billion gentle breezes buoy her body, caress her carapace, sweep her spiracles. She is warm. Safe. Together.

Light returns, a life lived large. No longer attenuated but attached; grounded in grace, carried by community, lifted in love.

She is one. She is many.

4

FOR NOW

BY ERIN JO ELDRY

A caterpillar does not anticipate her future
She does not sit on a leaf and gaze at the moon come midnight
Dreaming of wings with innocent expectation
Instead, she'll live in blissful ignorance of something greater than herself
Comfortable in an Earthly routine
Until succumbing to the will of the God that made her
Since her creation, she was destined for metamorphosis
To not understand what will eventually become of her
And we are both the same
I cannot in good honesty say that I conceive a future
How can I when I'm trapped in this prison of windowless brain cells?
Solitude in a cocoon made of tear-soaked sheets and stained cotton pajamas
Sentenced to looping memories that decay whatever's left
Downtrod from a shattered promise
Brokenhearted from the lie of a love eternal
Is this what our chrysalis was made to be?

A mental fog by the wicked we swore to love forever?
A lonesome hollow where sentience of the meek fades
to die?
So be it, then
I have no will to argue what's already been decided for me
Much as the caterpillar has no say in what has also been
chosen for her
What will be, will be
I'll melt into the ether
Suffer through the night
Sprout from what I was created to endure
And if there is a tomorrow?
Like those of the caterpillars soon to live as butterflies?
I'm sorry
I have no strength left to pray that mine will be as kind.

5

THE RASH

BY CHAYLEE MCCLEESE

I got into the front seat of my car and slammed the door shut. A cool droplet fell from the corner of my eye while I took off my school lanyard. My fingers picked through my clunky charms until I found the fob. I needed to get out of here. My slug bug rumbled to life as I turned the key in the ignition. I cranked the AC up, even though it couldn't save me from the summer heatwave or the doctor's words.

I am sorry to tell you this, but your ANA test came back positive. This is just something you will have to live with.

I threw my purple wallet into the cup holder. My driver's license was sticking out. Stephine Brant. Minor. Brown Eyes. 5'4. Birthdate 5/12/2008. The picture was of me, but I couldn't recognize myself anymore. My face was puffier now.

I backed out of the rheumatologist's parking lot, without a clue of where I was going. I forgot to plug the aux cord into my phone, so the radio turned on at full blast. The local station played the same annoying top 10 songs, but I tried to enjoy the music anyway. However, all I could hear was the doctor's words repeating in my head.

This is just something you will have to live with.

More tears blurred my sight, causing me to barely see the road's markings. I took a couple of random turns onto some side streets, unsure of what to do. Then, I caught a glimpse of a familiar place.

I pulled my car over to the curb of my old bus stop and put the gear in park. The sidewalk contained a metal bench and a non-working phone booth. My mom used to wait for me there every day after school. Even though she was in pain, she would smile and wave at me, yelling, *Stephie! I can't wait to hear about your day!* No matter how mundane my life was, she would ask me questions all the way back to our house. She wanted to know everything I did—from what I learned in each subject, to what I ate for lunch, to how I spent my recess time. The bus stop used to be busy and full of life. Now, it was rundown and abandoned.

I flipped the sun visor down and opened the mirror. My tears destroyed my foundation's coverage. The splotchy red rash that blanketed the area underneath my eyes and over my nose was lurid and irritated. I had seen it before. It was the same shape as my mother's rash. But I wasn't like her. I couldn't be. My slug bug's already confined walls began to close in on me. I jumped out of the front seat and went to sit on the bench.

When a slight breeze finally came, the dam holding my fears leaked. Tears fell hard and fast. I put my hands over my face, hoping no one was around to see the mess I had become.

I missed my mom. Nothing was the same without her, and she was the only one who would understand this.

There was something bright stuck in the crease of my car's hood. I rose, tucking my frizzy brown hair behind my ears, and walked over to it. Maybe it was a ribbon or a little girl's lost hair tie.

I carefully popped open the hood and placed the bright blob into the palm of my hand. It was a butterfly. The poor insect must have gotten too hot and crawled in. Unfortunately, it was dead, but everything about it was still in place. Its beautiful yellow and black wings were spread wide open. The creature's bottom trim shined blue and orange, and its antennas were upright. The butterfly was perfect. Just like my mom, even though they both were gone from this world, their impact remained.

I carried its lifeless body into my car and placed it on top of the dash. I took a deep breath and looked at myself in the mirror once again. Instead of seeing my mother's pain in the rash, I saw beautiful butterfly wings.

This is just something you will have to live with, the doctor had said.

Maybe I could live with this. My mom had. My fingers gravitated to the butterfly's wings. The touch transferred my mom's resilience onto me.

6

THE BUTTERFLY WING

BY HEATHER HASSIG

"What happened to it, Mama?"
My toddler asks.
She found the butterfly's wing
On the pavement
Papery thin
Iridescent colors
No body left to fly.

In preschool,
She learned about caterpillars,
And chrysalises,
And metamorphosis.
They hatched eggs,
Watched them every day,
Waited for them to emerge
Into a beautiful butterfly.

Then they released them.
The children watched with joy
When the delicate wings

Ascended into the sky.

In school, she learned
All of that.
But she didn't learn this part.

I have to find a way to tell her
About the end.
I have to find the words
To explain death,
And how beautiful things can break.

And how none of this lasts forever.

Except that joy.
Maybe the joy stays.

7

THE BOOK OF WINGS

BY A. N. GRIFFITH

The Book of Wings sat on Mom's shelf.

When I was five, I would stand on my tiptoes to sneak the book filled with preserved butterflies.

"Don't!" She'd swat my hand away. "There's nothing for you in there, AnnaMae."

Still, I'd risk a timeout to count the butterflies she'd collected. It was the one spot, the one thing, in our house that was beautiful.

Behind the broken toaster, mouse droppings were scattered like crumbs, and the counters served as fairgrounds for roaches eager to eat the moldy food that piled up.

"You could fry eggs with the grease in your hair," a classmate once told me. I didn't know how to tell him our water was cut off. Or how to explain to my teacher I wasn't dirty—just had nowhere to bathe but the creek.

Despite that, Mom's book and the shelf that housed it were always clean.

I considered burying her with it, but the thought of the butterflies never seeing light again was more unbearable than the thought of Mom being in the dark forever.

I could reach the book easily now.

In Mom's penmanship, the opening page read:

A butterfly for everything I need to change.

The first butterfly was an orange monarch. Below it, she'd written, *Finances.*

The second, a yellow one.

Happiness.

The third, red.

Love.

I skipped to the last page, my chest inexplicably heavy.

In the corner, in her faded script:

I wanted more for AnnaMae. She'll break her chrysalis. I never could.

8

BUTTERFLIES IN THE SNOW

BY SALLY LOTZ

Sometime after midnight, the snow stops and I peer out into the night. The city is silent, except for the howling of the wind between the buildings. Above me, something knocks and hammers in the storm, a loose shingle, or the metal bars on the fire escape. I can't tell. Streets are empty of the buses with advertisements for chewing gum and taxis that seem to only move by honking their horns. Gone is the endless stream of people, always hurrying along the sidewalk to get to wherever they are going. They're all home now, locked behind their doors, they don't see the snow, white and smooth like frosting on a cake, covering everything. And the yellow light of the street-lights twinkling as if it were Christmas. Or that everything is clean and smelling fresh, like laundry hung on the line to dry.

The snow started earlier in the day. At first, it came down slowly in giant fluffy flakes. They floated and drifted to the ground, where they melted. I caught them on my tongue. They tasted sweet, like the sugar cookies grandma used to make. The flakes became thicker and heavier as the day drew on, falling in sheets, piling up in corners and on ledges. And that's when I headed for my place, the narrow space between two buildings. The wind howled, and people, their heads bent, hurried to get home. I didn't mind at all. It was like winter back in Nebraska, where we'd sit on the long cold nights listening to the wind blow across the plain while we sat around the fireplace playing Uno or Monopoly, if Dad were up to it. Then we'd have popcorn from a big bowl, our fingers greasy with butter.

I wish for Nebraska and those times. But it was so long ago, and everyone is gone. There's no one to remember me, but I remember them. I pull Rex close and wrap us up in a quilt I'd found at the Salvation Army Thrift Store for $1.00. I'd chosen it not just because it was cheap and would keep me warm, but because of its pattern of stars in shades of blue. And because of the tiny butterfly patch sewn into the corner. The quilt and butterfly are both reminders of home when Mom and her friends quilted on our front porch. They shared colorful scraps of fabric while drinking tea from delicate cups with pale violet flowers painted onto the fragile porcelain. And my grandmother would appear from the kitchen with a tray of tiny sandwiches with the crusts removed. If my brother, Ben, and I were quiet, my grandmother would give us each a sandwich and a slice of cake–but only if we were very quiet.

Rex whimpers and wriggles before settling his head against my chest. His warm body against mine takes away some of the chill, but I'm still cold. The icy chill seeps in from the cement beneath me, the pieces of cardboard I'd laid out, not doing their job. I should have stayed at the shelter, but they wouldn't let Rex in, and I can't leave him alone.

Rex moves closer, as if he knows what I am thinking. I don't tell him how each breath hurts as the icy air hits my lungs and how my bones ache with cold.

"It's only a little cold. We've been through worse, and tomorrow, we'll be warm again," I say, patting his head. He pulls closer. "Tomorrow we'll have a big breakfast at the Community Kitchen."

Eventually, my eyelids grow heavy, and I drift off to sleep. I dream of warm beaches and coconut-scented sunscreen, and backyard picnics on the 4th of July with glasses of iced tea, and lemonade with thick slices of lemon, the sun bright and warm. I dream of chasing Ben through the tall grass and into the cornfield. Just the edge, because the cornfield was a place where a boy like Ben could get lost. I dream of riding Bay, my horse, along the dried river bed, and of the rain's fresh smell.

A CAR HORN WAKES ME. I shift but don't get up until Rex licks my chin and nudges me with his nose.

"Okay, I'm awake," I say, and wrap myself tighter in the quilt.

Rex stands, shaking off a layer of frost from his fur. He licks my hand and face again until I sit up. But I don't want to move. The dreams from last night linger in my head. They're always the same. I dream of home. Because after home comes darkness. Always the darkness. And I never dream of that. I can't let myself go there. It's done and I am here now, with Rex.

My dog barks, a playful bark, and tugs at the quilt.

"Okay, okay," I say, loosening the quilt.

There are no clouds in the sky, and the sun is so bright it lights up everything around me. I shield my eyes with my hand, and something blue flits near my face before landing on my knee. It stretches its wings, opening and closing them slowly. Then, just as fast as it landed, it takes off. I rub my eyes. It's far too cold for a butterfly. I must still be dreaming.

Rex barks, his nose pointed toward the sky, where another butterfly has joined the other. The two do a graceful fluttering dance, circling each other. Then, they dart away, down the narrow space between the buildings before disappearing around the corner.

"I guess I'm not seeing things," I say. "Grandma had a saying about blue butterflies. I wish I could remember it."

Rex tilts his head and barks, reminding me we have to hurry.

I shrug off the quilt and stand. Stretching my arms wide, I notice that my joints don't make their usual popping sounds for the first time in a while. It must be too cold for anything like that. I arrange myself like I do every morning by smoothing down my hair, tugging up my socks, and tightening my belt. I shake out my quilt, marveling again at the pattern of stars someone had sewn by hand. I wrap it around my shoulders and pull up my hood for extra warmth. Soon, Rex and I are on our way.

We step out from our home and onto the sidewalk. Around us, the city swarms with life. It's hard to believe how peaceful it had been a few hours ago when it was only Rex and me. The street is plowed, and banks of snow are piled at the curb. Somehow, I slept through it. The usual mix of traffic churns the snow into a gray slush. My heart races. It's later than I thought, and breakfast is only served until 8:30. I need something warm in my belly, and Rex does, too.

Another look around at the traffic and the people in their hurried walks tell me we're okay, but we don't have much time left.

"It's only five blocks, Rexie. We can do this," I say.

We make our way down the crowded sidewalk. No one seems to shift away from me today or look at me with sad eyes or disgust, like usual. It must be the cold. Rex whines. I am going too fast for him. I slow down at the entrance to the glass-fronted office building. Here, I would normally slip between the big cement planters filled with shrubs covered in burlap to keep them from freezing, to get warm. It's the best place to stay hidden from Tony, the doorman. He doesn't like it when we rest here; he says I scare people. Today, though, I'm not cold. And oddly, Tony doesn't seem to mind seeing me as I near. He doesn't shoo me away. Instead, he reaches down and pats Rex on the head. He speaks gently to Rex, even giving him a treat from his pocket. My stomach rumbles, calling for breakfast. I thank him and move on our way.

"We have to hurry, Rex. Breakfast will be over soon," I say, and Rex follows, looking back over his shoulder at Tony. "He's just being nice because of the cold. Tomorrow he'll go back to normal."

Rex and I weave our way through the throng of people and wait at the corner for the crosswalk sign to flash white. That's when I spot it, there on the other side, in the snowbank left by the plow, a single white glove. It's the same color as the snow. I almost missed it. When I bend to pick it up, a cab nearly runs me over. I jump out of the way and wave my fist. Rex barks. It does no good.

I examine the glove closely. It's made of suede. The fingers are long and delicate. Fur—fake, I hope—lines the opening. There isn't a mark on it. I slip my gnarled fingers inside. It is an expensive glove; someone is missing it. One glove can keep me warm, though. But it's not mine. I never take things that don't belong to me. That's something Momma always taught me. Perhaps whoever lost it, isn't missing it yet.

"Come on, Rex." I pat his head and continue down the next block, darting in and around the people who still refuse to move. I check the hands of those at the bus stop, or those who wait for a cab or their Uber. Everyone seems to be wearing two gloves.

A gust of wind blows, and my hood flops back. I don't feel the cold.

It's funny; I hadn't really felt the cold all morning. Because I am already frozen, I laugh.

"Almost there, Rex," I say.

I can already taste the hot coffee and the warm fluffy pancakes topped with syrup and loaded with mounds of butter. It's what we have every Wednesday. If it's a lucky Wednesday, there'll be fruit like bananas or apples. Always bruised and cast away, just like those of us at the shelter.

I spot a woman at the bus stop, wearing a white scarf. I stop and hold the glove up, asking if it belongs to her. She looks through me as if I am not there. What did I expect? That's how they always look at me. Her short, stubby fingers, I see, are already covered in red gloves. The white suede would never fit her. I move on, Rex at my heels.

Then I see her, standing at the center of the sidewalk, halfway down the block at the entrance to the Community Kitchen. The crowd parts around the woman, not stopping at the obstacle in their path. I can see her clearly, clearer than I've seen in years. It's like I had my glasses again. She wears a white hat with a ball of fur on the tip, the same as the glove. I call and wave, but she doesn't appear to hear me. She is looking down as if she has lost something. Her glove?

Rex nudges me to go, and I do. Time seems to shift. One moment, I am at the corner, and the next, I am standing in front of her. I hadn't even taken a step. Her skin glistens like the snow at night, and her coat is white suede like the glove, and it sparkles in a beam of sunlight. The sidewalk at her feet is dry. Rex lies down with his chin in his paws. The woman, taller than she looked from far away, shifts her gaze to me. Her clear blue eyes investigate me, not through me. I know she can tell what I am thinking. Her lips, the color of the red roses in Momma's garden, turn up into a smile, and warmth starts in my chest, fanning out across my body. I cannot look away.

I hold up the glove. Surely, it's hers. She nods and takes it from me before slipping it onto her long, delicate fingers. She holds her hands out to me, her palms facing upward. I look from the suede gloves to her face. Her eyes are full of kindness and warmth. Again, she says nothing.

Behind her, the same two butterflies I'd seen earlier float in the air. They flutter their wings, catching the sunlight as they dash and dart around her. Then, I remember all about the blue butterfly, what my grandmother had said.

They take the burdens of your soul. It means you're about to leave something behind and gain freedom. A new life, like being reborn, she'd said.

Rex sits up and barks playfully like he used to when he was a puppy and nudges me again. I take the woman's hands. My dirty fingers, the nails broken, and bones gnarled, don't seem so ugly anymore. My skin tingles. Warmth envelops me like a giant hug, something I haven't felt since before the darkness. As the sounds of the city fade, I hear the voices of my past, my mom, Gran, Gramps, Dad,

Ben, and even Bay. I see myself chasing after a kite and kissing Ronnie behind the barn in fifth grade. I smell the grass as I run through it barefoot and feel the sun's warmth on my shoulders as I walk to school with my best friends, Anna Marie and K. Just K, we called her, and it always made us laugh.

The summer and laughter fade, and the sky turns grey. The dark place. My heart races. I don't want to go there.

The woman whispers my name, and squeezes my hands tighter, but not so that it hurts. And the grey fog shifts and fades away. There are more butterflies now, too many for me to count. Where did they come from? Still holding her hands, I feel light, with no pain in my hips or back, and I realize my feet are no longer touching the ground.

Rex, my mind races. But he is by my side, his head rests against my thigh.

"It's going to be okay. Everyone is waiting," the woman speaks, her soft voice filling my head, her lips unmoving. I feel her words and know they are true.

As we go higher and reach the tops of the buildings, I look down one last time. On the dry spot of the sidewalk, my starry quilt lay in a heap. The people move like ants around it. Frank comes out the doors of the Community Kitchen, stopping at my quilt. With his hands on his hips, he looks around and then picks it up. He holds it for a moment, his head bent as if saying a prayer, then folds it into a neat square before going back inside. He knows it's my quilt. Everyone who matters knows it's mine.

Frank doesn't look up. No one on the street does. They are all focused on getting to where they are going, never stopping, never noticing anything but themselves. If they did look up, they'd see an angel, holding onto the hands of an old lady, wrinkled and weathered, dirty from living on the street, her dog at her side, and a trail of blue butterflies circling them all.

They'd see the dark parts of my soul washed away, just like my grandmother had said. But maybe it's better they don't. The dark parts are ugly and don't matter anymore—at least not where I am going.

9

A CATERPILLAR GIRL

BY RUSSELL CHAMBERLAIN

In a realm between twilight and dawn, I found myself wandering through the humid southern city that wore its age like a faded velvet cloak. An autumnal pallor streaked by my eyes with each passing building wet with decay. A place steeped in folklore, parties, music, and fever. A place of jazz and vampires drunk with the idea of Bourbon Street. The crowded avenue, slick with the after-glow of rain, shimmered with life, yet felt utterly forgotten in the frenzy—all color without context, all laughter without sound. Mouths opened wide, but I could not hear them. A strange enchantment hung in the air, a thin veil between reality and surreal. I walked past the well-lit store-fronts, but I was neither here nor there—a transient soul caught in the gentle grasp of the twilight hour, when the light began to fade, and shadows twisted into whimsical shapes. All of this was to say that I thought I was dreaming in that old French city.

The vision was clear, and now the sounds filled the empty spaces, where previously there had been none. The streets echoed with laughter, the kind of laughter that might belong to spirits playing just out of sight. Music floated through the air, a harmonious mix of distant melodies and the soft strumming of unseen guitars. Somewhere in that cacophony, a kazoo chimed in, a whimsical sound that was both absurd and oddly beautiful.

I strolled along, my mind a tempest of thoughts, scattering like fallen leaves in a brisk autumn wind. That's when I saw an impossibly large caterpillar crawling along a cobbled path that shimmered with the remnants of a rain-soaked day. Faintly luminescent, it was both an invitation and a riddle, beckoning me closer with its slow, deliberate movements.

"Do you remember the dreams you left behind?" it murmured, a honeyed whisper that seemed to weave through the air like smoke. "Or have you wrapped yourself too tightly in the webs of your own making?"

I paused. What a curious creature to pose such questions, nestled amidst this contradictory scene. Had my dreams truly escaped me? Was I wrapped in the tangled mess of life, a creature of my design? My time was short; had I squandered it?

"I am not a child anymore," I replied, an unsteady defiance edging my voice. "I embrace what I've become, however strange or lost."

The caterpillar laughed a sound that was scratchy and inhuman. "And yet here you are, still searching, balancing on the precipice of who you might yet be. Would you rather let the ghost of your past haunt your splendid present?"

With a flourish of its many legs, the caterpillar beckoned me forward, teasing out a smile I hadn't worn in ages. I walked alongside the curious creature, my heart heavy with memories that whispered of freedom, rebellion, and the reckless abandonment of youth. I remembered the nights spent adorned in the excitement of dreams, my face painted like a canvas of punk rock, or glam, vibrantly resisting conformity.

"Would you trade the comfort of your known prison for the chaos of endless possibility?" the caterpillar chimed, guiding me past children running in a flurry of color, their joy like bells ringing in the dark night. They ran through the crowded streets cutting a path for us. Flowers braided through their hair, their innocence spun magic into the air, helping to lift the weight of adulthood from my weary shoulders. I looked at the second story balconies just above my head with people whooping and cheering for the throng below. These people had left their cares behind, perhaps I could, too.

But lurking beneath that enchantment, a chilling breeze brushed against my neck. The caterpillar's words circled in my mind, echoing through the paths of memory. "The night would turn to dust, just like the people who filled these streets," it reminded me, as if warning me against the inexorable march of time.

"No," I countered, a flicker of protest in my heart. I had come too far to be swayed by the specter of despair. It was day again as warmth spilled over the horizon, illuminating the path ahead. With all its flaws and wonders, the city opened before me like a treasure trove. The colors breathed a different kind of life in the daylight. Sweet scents of flowers and pastries drifted through the air, nostalgia simmered like preserves on a stove, each jar a fragment of stories waiting to be unearthed from my mind. I felt wonderment in that moment, as the caterpillar and I rounded the next street corner.

A parade stretched out before us—a wondrous procession of life, laughter, and joy. Flamboyant floats glided by, each adorned with vibrant flowers, and the beat of drums pulsed in tune with hope blooming within me. My heart surged as the music wrapped around us, a reminder that magic could be found each moment, even when draped in the shadows of nagging despair.

In that beautiful chaos of sound and color, fragments of my youth returned, buoying me like the feathers of a thousand dreams. The caterpillar—once a looming figure taunted me—now seemed simply curious. Perhaps it was a guide, a creature of wisdom pushing me toward the magic that lingered, waiting to be seized.

As I moved forward, the caterpillar by my side, I realized that beauty thrived beneath the fading veil of time, in the dance of the present, where love pulsed like the rhythm of life and the longing for what was and what might yet be interwoven like the petals of blossoming flowers. The night, once uncertain, felt like the voice of new beginnings—the promise that in every ending, there is a chance for rebirth.

I felt a fresh sense of discovery. Love surrounded me in the streets, filling the air with joy. Life felt new, and I hoped this feeling would be real and lasting. I wanted the world to be free and alive, filled with beautiful smiles. Suddenly, the caterpillar wrapped around my leg, causing panic, yet a strange calm washed over me.

"You will break free," the caterpillar whispered, and I remembered that everything was beautiful as it wrapped around me like a cocoon.

"I don't want to be afraid," I said weakly.

"No need," it said. "You can be like me, more beautiful than you ever knew." I heard the voice, but it faded as I became aware of my blankets once more and realized that everything was beautiful. A fleeting thought like the youth I dreamt of in the late morning. My head was not moving, and my eyes stayed fixed on the passing sky outside my window. Each cloud was a memory I didn't want to let go of.

10

A MOTH TO A FLAME

BY KELLY GRABOVAC

Pythia's limbs trembled with each step she took toward the goddess' throne.

The seat had been crafted by the sea, thousands of small stones and minerals forged into one unbreakable shell. Shimmering hues of translucent gold and foaming blues flashed along the scalloped edges of the clam husk. But instead of a pearl, the goddess Aphrodite nestled into the center, a frown pulling down her full lips.

Pythia's steadying breath echoed as a rasping cough in the cavernous space. The crashing waves beyond the cave did little to muffle the nervous sound, panic sending her knees cracking against the wet ground.

"I must say, I've never had such a foul creature approach me." Aphrodite cocked her head, a curtain of silken gold sliding over her bare shoulder. "What are you?"

Though the words did not surprise her, Pythia's heavy wings twitched with agitation. She had always been a *what*. Her sister, well, she had always been a *who*.

"I am Pythia, daughter of King Theras."

Aphrodite's lip curled at her sire's name, encouraging Pythia to continue.

"And I have come to make a bargain with you, goddess."

The deity, beauty incarnate, stood, and the sea at the cave's mouth seemed to quiet. The entire world took a breath, time bowing to the goddess. Aphrodite looked down at her the same way her sister did. Pythia gazed upon her curse—to always share company with those that outshone her.

"Your sire perverts my temple." The goddess' slender fingers curled into fists. "And he dares send this creature to barter with me?"

Pythia pulled back the gray membranes, flattening them against her back. The fur coating them tracked goosebumps against her pale skin. "King Theras did not send me. I have come here against him. And against my sister." Boldly, bravely, Pythia rose to her feet. "You have heard of Psyche, I believe."

The earth beneath Pythia's feet trembled. She fought the curve of her lips, enjoying the shared sentiment of bitter rage.

But the goddess' trilling laugh cut through the tension. "You? You stand there and claim to be the sister of Psyche?" Aphrodite stepped forward, her exposed curves finding the soft light of dawn. "Impossible."

"It is true—"

"Psyche has stolen my worshippers. And I doubt anyone has knelt before you."

Pythia had spent years receiving similar insults, and still, she could not stop her jaw from clenching. A moment passed before she managed a calm answer. "I share one sire with Psyche—King Theras. But Psyche has heritage with the naiads, and I have heritage with the dryads."

"Half-sister, then." Aphrodite's ocean-blue irises swam with a vengeance only immortals could perfect. "Don't tell me half-truths, monster."

Pythia had never considered herself half of anything. She was nothing.

"Psyche has wronged us both. I would like to help you even the scales."

Another long beat of silence. Pythia strained to keep her heavy wings flat, lest they insult the goddess. A cool breeze played with her hair, the gray locks a continuation of the horrid fur that covered her rounded membranes.

"Very well, I will hear your offer," Aphrodite said, and the pressure in Pythia's chest loosened as the goddess sat back on her throne. "But if I don't like it, I may do humanity a favor and rid this world of you."

Death was no longer the worst fate she could imagine. "Psyche has had many suitors, as you know." Again, the goddess' eyes flashed. "In order to choose which deserved my sister's hand, my father went to Delphi. There, the oracles spoke a prophecy. Despair, King Theras, they chanted. Your daughter will marry a beast even the gods fear. Dress her in funeral clothes and take her to the tallest rock spire in the kingdom. There, she shall meet her doom."

The churning waters sang a mournful harmony while Pythia steadied herself again.

"My father refused to accept this fate for Psyche. In front of his council, in front of his daughters, he lamented—how could one so..." Pythia swallowed, then began again. "How could one so *beautiful* be fated to marry a beast? The oracles clearly did not mean Psyche. And then my father raised his finger at me."

The memories stirred the thick burdens she carried, raising them off her back. Pythia could not fight it, just as she had not been able to fight the absolute concurrence the congregation had proclaimed. Not even Psyche had risen to save her.

"Tonight, my sister will walk with me as my handmaiden. Atop the rock spire, I will wait for the beast to take me away." Pythia forced herself to hold the goddess' stare. "Psyche is heavily guarded, day and night. But I will convince her to leave her guard for our final moment together." Surely, Psyche's guilt would encourage her to accept her last wish. "I will kill my sister, Aphrodite. You have seen how the people worship her beauty. Once she is gone, they will return to your temple. And all I ask for in return is for your blessing."

A slow, saccharine smile widened her unearthly features. "You wish to be beautiful, don't you, little moth?"

The goddess demanded no half-truths. "Yes."

"Eros." Aphrodite snapped her fingers, a thunderclap against Pythia's ears.

A flash of light blinded Pythia and sent her heavy wings folding around her in defense. The membranes' shadow helped her eyes adjust. She had always felt safer in the dark. And yet...

Pythia pulled her wings back and took in the strong form stretching to the left of Aphrodite's throne, nothing but a loincloth covering the god's golden skin. Eros's stretch sent his wings reaching toward the heavens, every white feather perfect, unstained. The untainted membranes emitted a soft glow, like the rest of him, the mixture of light and heat quickly filling the space around them.

Pythia had never been able to resist the light.

Instinctively, she took a step toward him.

"You called, mother?" The god spared Pythia a single

glance, and her stomach curled against the disgust she found in his golden eyes.

"Yes. I've just struck a deal with this creature." Aphrodite lifted a lazy finger toward her. "It seems you are needed at a wedding tonight."

Eros turned away from Pythia, only to roll his eyes at his mother. "Another? I'm getting rather bored."

Aphrodite snorted. "This isn't another prince and virgin. This is her wedding, with a beast."

"Surely, you don't wish for this insect to create more?" Eros took a step toward Pythia. Though she recognized the meaning behind his words, the decrease in space between them tightened her skin and sent her feeble heart fluttering. His light. His heat. An aurora only a god could conjure, and one her lesser instincts could not resist. Need pounded in her blood.

"Of course not," the goddess said. "This one will kill her handmaiden. Psyche—I'm sure I've mentioned her before."

Eros frowned. "Jealousy does not look good on you, mother."

Aphrodite ignored her son. "And you will kill the groom. Apparently, the monster is making even the faithful servants of Apollo question our power."

"Ah. Now that—" The golden god snapped his fingers, and a long bow appeared in his hand. "Is a cause I can put my bow behind."

"I thought so." Aphrodite looked Pythia up and down, storm-filled gaze catching on the wings peeking over her shoulders. Just as Pythia could not keep her eyes off her son's magnificent wings. "Meet her at the tallest rock spire in Greece at dusk."

"Pythia," she whispered.

The goddess continued on. "You will report to me if this creature fulfills her side of the bargain."

"Pythia."

"And if the moth falters, I expect you to finish the job." Aphrodite fixed a hard gaze on Eros.

"My name is Pythia." Despite the volume, her voice still wobbled, shaky echoes holding none of the confidence that she had intended the declaration to carry to the immortals.

"Do not be late, creature."

The god of love did not spare her a glance before disappearing in a flash of light.

And it was all she could do to not leap after him.

PYTHIA PACED the edge of the tall grass, colorful robes contrasting with the dull hues of her wings, skin, and hair. Though the membranes growing from her back sat heavier than her sister's, Pythia spread them out, anxiety keeping the patterned, furry flesh held high. Hues of orange and purple painted the sky, a vibrant welcome for both the moon and the all too smug handmaiden at her side.

"You look radiant, sister," Psyche preened from her perch on a stone to her right.

The lie set Pythia's teeth together and scratched at her ears. Every god, old and new, understood that Psyche only spoke of herself.

For the world withered underneath her ethereal figure.

The limitations of mortality bended to accommodate her lustrous features.

Every natural color failed to imitate the glistening glow of the delicate membranes stretching from her back.

Unlike Pythia's, Psyche's wings had been crafted by

membrane so thin it looked like sea glass. The near-translucent skin stretched to points above her rounded shoulders, held high not from anxiety, but from pride. Psyche had never felt the need to hide her effervescent wings, or shimmering hair. Not when people cried for her to reveal them. Not when their father begged for a moment with his daughter's nymph-like presence.

Pythia tucked her thick, gray wings into her back, a single glance at Psyche's blue and silver wings pushing her entire being into the ground in shame. The gentle breeze seemed to sing the same tune—unworthy, unwanted, unlovable.

The dozen guards King Theras forced to accompany Psyche failed to evaluate their surroundings, every gaze transfixed on the fluttering wings that made the stars seem like shit stains on a babe's first cloth.

"I do not want to be alone for my final flight as a maiden." Pythia pushed her shoulders back, digging for the same arrogance Psyche found naturally. "Escort me to my groom."

Psyche sighed, swinging her braid over her shoulder, pale blue robes moving around her curves as a steady wind caressed the sea. "Father won't like it. He told me not to leave my guards."

"Father has not even come to see his eldest daughter married." Pythia waved her hand at the grassy descent behind them, an empty hill. Not one member of their kingdom had come to see her off. She may be a monster, she may be ugly, but she still held the title of royalty. "Come with me up the rock. Hold my hand."

It took more courage than she cared to admit to make the demand. She had no experience with deceit; furtive glances revealed no sign of Eros, and she had looked for him since midday. The light that had accompanied his exit, the heat he had left in his wake... Pythia swallowed against the surge of desire that battled the nerves in her veins.

"I don't know." Psyche rose, and the swish of her hips had each guard stumbling back, awakening from the stupor she had put them in.

"It will most likely be the last time you see me," Pythia pushed. There was some truth in her statement, at least.

The rocky spire loomed over their heads, a mess of jagged edges and sheer cliffs. But height had never been their disadvantage; despite the differences in their wings, both she and Psyche had found flight with ease. How the beast would manage it, she did not consider. What did it matter, when it was due to die, too?

"You have called for many favors today," Psyche complained. But Pythia knew her sister's tells. The downward tilt of her eyes, the thin line her plump lips formed. Guilt, for the sister that had taken the horrible destiny Psyche had been due. Psyche's sparkling wings threw the last of the sun's rays into her guards' faces as she turned. "Remain here. I will escort my sister to her groom."

"Yes, princess."

Pythia restrained from rolling her eyes at the devoted reply, a response she had never earned from her father's men. The guards did not even spare her a glance, every stance of attention trained on the beautiful woman before them.

And she could not deny that Psyche's otherworldly appearance did not affect her.

Pythia found herself staring, drinking in the slender legs peeking out of the folds of her robes, the chain of diamonds that failed to sparkle as brightly as the silver-blue wings. Psyche's eyes—blue, like the sky of a young summer day—raked her over, and Pythia had to force down her own cry of gratitude that the princess spent any time appraising her. Such beauty did not belong on a mortal woman.

Pythia had known that when she approached Aphrodite. Easy to play the strings of jealousy, when she had been choked by them her entire life.

"The sun sets, Pythia." Indeed, a gloom settled over their surroundings, but somehow did not touch Psyche. "Let us go to your husband."

"Let's." Pythia reached toward her sister. Refused to shrink underneath the look of disgust Psyche could not disguise quick enough. Still, her younger sister found the courage to grab her hand, and together, they stretched their wings and launched into the sky.

Gods, it always felt glorious, to become weightless. To leave behind the mortal world and join the immortals in the sky. Twilight covered their ascent up the spire, a gentle transition from Helios to Selene. Despite their differences, her wings flapped in perfect rhythm with Psyche's, each beat a harmony they had found together, throughout the years.

The wind ripped at the top of the spire, nearly forcing them off course. But together, they managed a soft landing, sheer end to the spire providing a thin ledge. Pythia released Psyche's hand, scarlet bridal robes billowing around her, mixing with her sister's garb.

Psyche swallowed, a tell of her nervousness. It rekindled the rageful fire that continually smoldered within Pythia. Did her sister not understand that this wedding was supposed to be her fate? Did Psyche not care that a member of her own family took her place? The young princess stepped toward the ledge. "I wish you luck on your nuptials, sister."

The simmering fire erupted with volcanic fury.

"Won't you wait with me, *sister*?" The honorific hissed

from between Pythia's clenched teeth. "Won't you look upon the beast that you should have married?"

Psyche's twitching demeanor melted into the arrogance she always wore. "We both know I was never destined to marry this monster. Accept your fate, Pythia."

Psyche turned away, exposing a full tapestry of utter perfection.

The unhindered display of beauty snapped Pythia's hold on sanity.

She roared, lunging toward the ungrateful monster blessed with nothing other than a pleasing skin. Pythia grabbed two fistfuls of delicate, shimmering membrane, and tore.

And tore.

And tore.

Psyche's screams did not deter her. Pythia focused only on the glittering shreds of wings fluttering to the harsh rock beneath them. Each tendril of blue and silver hid the rough red and brown earth, until it gave the illusion that Pythia stood on sea and cloud. Psyche fell to her knees, as if she had finally learned how to bow to the gods.

Pythia swore she heard Aphrodite's chuckle on the wind.

But it was Eros who appeared, a flash of light halting her frantic motions. Pythia released the last handfuls of Psyche's wings, wide gaze set on the fire that crafted the god of love. As the brightness faded, the heat did not. The sculpted god held a bow, flaming arrow nocked.

The flickering fire sucked Pythia in, froze her entirely. Psyche sobbed at her feet, beads of blood running down her back, staining the handmaiden's robes.

Eros said nothing, frowning at the ribbons of wings scattered about. But the promise she had made to Aphrodite faded to the back of her mind as she remained transfixed on the flaming god.

Desire, lust, love. She had experienced those feelings before. None of them had been reciprocated. Still, she found herself stepping toward the god, her entire body trembling with need.

A guttural snarl rippled through the young night.

The sound forced her stomach to flip, trailed goosebumps down her arms. The monster did not sound eager for a bond of marriage, but for a meal.

"That's my cue." Eros leapt into the air, feathered wings snapping out behind him. He backflipped into the deep shadows, a sickening sound of slithering growing closer.

The disappearance of the god and his flaming arrow finally broke the spell that had taken over Pythia's body. She snapped her attention back to her sister, who crawled away.

"I hope you meet your groom in the underworld."

Pythia shoved her sister off the spire's edge.

Her roar followed Psyche into the dark pit beneath them, a cry filled with years of indignities. The mocking Psyche had performed before their court, the solitude her father had deemed worthy of her station. The utter acceptance that the only one worthy of a horrible fate was Pythia.

All because of the dull, hideous membranes marking her back.

Psyche's screams ended the same moment a snap echoed through the night, and Pythia knew the bargain was complete.

For her wings molted, gray and black fur falling atop of Psyche's shredded membranes. In an instant, Pythia felt lighter. Free.

She pulled her wings around her, back no longer straining with effort, and gasped.

The thick, colorless flesh had been replaced by thin panels of glorious orange and silken black. The two colors fell into each other, effortlessly, the former a stunning imitation of the setting sun, the latter glittering, a tapestry of the night sky. The rounded edges melted into flirty tips. Beauty incarnate, stretching proud from her back.

"Thank you." Pythia sent her fervent whisper to the heavens, just as an ear-splitting roar shattered the night. An eerie silence followed it, the second sound of death that evening.

For a moment, only the moon witnessed her new body. Pythia spun atop the rock spire, enjoying the weightlessness that engulfed her.

No more heavy, horrid wings.

No more arrogant, selfish sister.

No more monstrous, prophesied groom.

The silvery glow of Selene faded behind Eros's fiery radiance. The god stood before her, a flaming arrow nocked in his bow. She didn't spot a scratch on him, and as no foul creature emerged from the shadows, she knew the beast had been slain.

Despite her transformation, her instincts screamed at her to approach. Gaze transfixed on the warm light, she took an unconscious step toward him. And another. A small part of her recognized that she treaded over the remnants of her wings, her sister's, but a larger part of her could not resist the god any longer.

"What do you think?" She took another step toward him. A gold curl of his hair fell over his forehead with a cock of his head.

"I think you are lucky you did not have to marry that serpent." To her surprise—and elation—he took a step toward her. Need made her mouth dry, the entire world narrowing to the flickering flame the god did not put out.

"What do you think of me?" Pythia outstretched her hand, trembling fingers entering Eros's space. His heat. She waited for the recoil that always followed her actions, but it did not come.

Eros raised his eyebrows. "You dare touch a god?"

"My sister spited the gods." She breathed the confession, flaming arrow so close to her flesh she felt the fire's bite. It only made her crave more. "I do not. All I want is..."

A touch. A taste. To sit in his light and heat, burning, forever.

"You may have metamorphosized on the outside, little butterfly." A wicked grin split the god's beautiful features. "But your soul... well, that did not change."

Eros's gaze dipped to the tattered wings beneath them.

"And it is ugly."

The god of love snapped up his bow, and Pythia's world ended in a flash of glorious fire.

11

WINGS OF SILK

BY RILEY KLABUNDE

The wings were beautiful. Even I could admit that. They shimmered in the morning light, the sun shining through the gossamer silk of lavender and gold like stained glass. With every step Yara took, they fluttered behind her, trembling along with her as she moved closer to the village square.

Today was Choosing Day.

To everyone else, this was a celebration—an auspicious time meant for joyous blessings. The day a chosen girl entered the woods to please the forest spirit, and the village would have another year of prosperity. This year, Yara, the person I cared about most in all the world, had been selected as the lucky bride.

The square had been dressed in the finest silks and floral arrangements. Petals floated in the air, released from hollow glass spheres by hidden strings. Children laughed as they danced around the fountain, butterfly masks of every color slipping from their innocent faces as they skipped to the beat of cheerful flutes and drums. The air smelled of nectar and burnt sugar.

I stood near the edge of the crowd, my hands clenched on the hem of my too-thin shawl. My own wings, the ones I had worked on for months of stolen hours, were hidden beneath my cloak, wrapped in canvas and copper wire as my heart thudded like a war drum in my chest.

I couldn't tear my gaze from Yara as she climbed the stone steps of the Sanctum of Wings, the breeze teasing the edge of her ceremonial gown, dyed the same lavender and gold as her butterfly wings and enchanted to glow faintly. With her hair woven with flowers and her face painted as a blushing bride, she was as radiant as the rising sun behind her.

More beautiful than I had ever seen her, and more devastating than I could ever imagine. Yara looked like a fairy queen come to life.

I wanted to scream.

I knew Yara didn't believe in the old stories any more than I did. We had laughed about them and terrorized the younger girls after dark. But when our turn came to stand before the elders, and it was her name that was called, she bowed her head, bit her tongue, and did not scream as they painted her feet with gold and called it a blessing.

It was never called what it was.

A sacrifice.

My stomach churned at the thought of Yara as that sacrifice, bile rising in my throat.

"Iris." A familiar hand gripped my arm. My mother, pale and wide-eyed, whispered furiously in my ear. "Don't look at her like that. You'll make them suspicious."

"I'm not looking at *her*," I lied through my clenched teeth. "I'm looking at the gate behind her."

Beyond Yara, the great iron gate stood closed. Vines

crept along its edges like grasping fingers, and rust clung to the bars in the shape of old bloodstains. I was always shocked at how no one ever opened it except on Choosing Day.

No one ever came back through.

The elders began to chant, low and melodic, while the rest of the village fell into a reverent silence. Yara faced the gate, raising her arms as robed figures stepped forward with silver keys. I wondered if I was the only one to see that her hands shook so hard she was vibrating or to notice the tears that stained her cheeks.

Something inside me snapped like a fraying thread.

Yara had always been there for me. She'd braid my hair with wild mint during the summer months or golden leaves in the autumn. She hated cinnamon but loved the smell of books. She would dare me to climb the tallest tree on the eastern ridge and be waiting for me at the bottom when I would only make it halfway up. Her laughter still echoed in my ears. I wanted to grab her, shake her, and scream, *Don't go, don't be next.*

But it was too late.

When the gate opened with a groan like the forest exhaling, I turned and stumbled away before breaking into a run. My heart shattered into a thousand pieces as I ran through the market stalls, down the hill, past the old chapel where the windows had long since been boarded up.

No one stopped me.

They were all too busy watching the butterfly walk into the woods.

I didn't return home.

Instead, I took the back path. The one that wound behind the chapel ruins and past the edge of the orchard, where the trees grew too crooked and the ground sank too soft beneath your feet. My shawl slipped from my shoulders as I ran. But I didn't care, it wasn't like I needed it anymore. By the time I reached the forest's edge, the village bell was ringing. One note. Two. Then a third and final toll.

The gate had closed, and Yara was gone.

I froze where I stood, staring up at the clear sky. Silence pressed in until all I could hear was my heartbeat echoing. A sound clawed up my throat, half-breath, half-cry, and broke apart in my mouth. Then nothing, only the wind.

The Whispering Wood loomed before me, tall and silver-veined, branches arched like cathedral ceilings. Fog clung to the roots like old breath. The leaves barely rustled, but I heard their whispers—the soft murmurings in a language I didn't understand.

Villagers said to stay out of the woods, that the trees would watch and wait. That the forest kept what it wanted. But they had been sending girls into it for generations. Pretty girls with obedient smiles and trembling hands. Girls who were told they'd be made into something *divine*.

Maybe they were or maybe they weren't. But I had seen the so-called divinity on Yara's face, and it looked a lot like fear.

Letting out a shaky breath, I unrolled the canvas bundle from beneath my cloak.

My wings were not beautiful. They did not shimmer, nor did they gently float through the air. They were jagged and heavy, made from scavenged metal, shards of glass, and wire pulled from the bones of dead machines. I'd painted them in blood reds, dusky purples, and golds so bright they nearly hurt to look at, just so they could stand out.

Forging them in fury and soldering them with spit and fire, I had made them with my own hands.

I slipped the harness over my shoulders and adjusted the leather straps with practiced fingers. The wings clicked into place with a sharp, mechanical snap. They didn't flutter or glow with beauty or grace. Instead, they *rang,* low and metallic, the way steel sings when it remembers fire.

I stepped into the trees.

The forest swallowed me in silence.

Behind me, the wind had moved. Birds had chirped. Somewhere, water had rushed through the creek. But inside the forest, the air was heavy and thick with quiet. It wasn't just still, it was *listening.* The ground beneath my feet pulsed with a heartbeat not my own.

I will not be afraid. I had come with a purpose, one I had spent weeks planning. I would save Yara, and we would be free together somewhere far away from our wretched village.

A worn path wound like ribbon through roots and stones, and I followed it without a thought. The trees leaned closer the farther I walked, their trunks spiraling with pale moss and markings like runes half-burned away. Occasionally, a butterfly passed me, silent and strange, its wings made of smoke or stars or something in between.

It took time to notice the bones. Tiny, bird-like shapes curled into roots. A ribcage lodged in the crook of a branch. A child's shoe with the lace still tied. They didn't feel like warnings, more like offerings to the unseen.

My skin chilled, and my throat tightened, but I told myself to keep walking, one foot in front of the other. *I will not be afraid.*

I pressed onward, the straps of my wings biting into my shoulders. My heartbeat throbbed against the wires. While a shiver traced down my spine, though not from cold. Power thrummed in the very air around me, while whispers of pain, some fresh and new, some as old as the trees themselves, filled my ears.

I reached a clearing at midday, but within the confines of the forest, the world appeared at twilight. A thick fog blocked any light from coming through, and nothing made a sound. The trees parted in a perfect circle, their trunks arched inward like a woven cage. In the middle of the clearing, a ring of mushrooms bloomed in shades of violet and black. I wondered if this was what I had come for, if this was where I would have my answers.

At the center of the ring hung a single cocoon. It dangled from a twisted silver branch, swaying despite the stillness in the air. Massive, longer than I was tall, and glowing faintly as if something inside still dreamed. Threads of iridescent silk shimmered like veins through its surface.

The cocoon pulsed as I stepped forward. Every instinct told me to stop, yet my body leaned closer, caught between dread and fascination.

My wings hummed in response, a discordant vibration rippling through my bones. Then came a voice. Eerie and echoing through my mind rather than spoken aloud.

Another girl. Another promise. Another lie.

I stumbled back, scanning the shadows. The forest stayed silent. But something moved behind the trees. Wings larger than my body beat in a slow, deliberate rhythm.

I swallowed hard.

"I didn't come to offer myself," I whispered. "I came to find my friend. To find the others. I seek the truth."

Silence.

Then laughter. Dry as autumn leaves, soft as ash. The sound sent a chill down my spine.

You came with wings of glass, child. What do you think you'll do? Fly?

My jaw clenched.

"No," I said. "I came to break them."

The forest exhaled, the cocoon stilled, and all around me, butterflies rose from the ground—hundreds of them. Wings tattered and frayed, glowing faintly like embers in the dark.

Parting like mist, they dissolved into motes of light as *she* stepped from the shadows.

The spirit appeared like a memory too long buried. Tall, barefoot, and wrapped in tattered folds of silk, her enormous wings, black-veined and shimmering, pulsed with threads of light that were dozens, no hundreds, of souls.

Her face was... *wrong*. Not monstrous nor beautiful. Just *many*. Lips that flickered through expressions not her own. Eyes that changed color with every blink. Hair like strands of moonlight and ash. A face stitched together from stolen identities.

Yara's eyes, Elayne's lips, my own sister's cheekbones. The familiar features broke my heart piece by piece as I recognized the faces of the girls I had watched disappear into the woods year after year.

The spirit smiled a toothy grin at me, the sharpness of her pointed teeth giving it a sinister leer. "You came willingly. How rare. Most are given, yet you gave." This time, when she spoke, it was aloud. The sound reverberated as if it were many voices talking as one. My skin prickled, and for a moment I couldn't tell if it was awe or fear that hollowed my chest.

"No." My voice trembled, but I did not look away from her unblinking gaze. "I came to take them back."

She tilted her head as if listening to a note only she could hear, while she smirked like I had said something she found amusing.

"So sure of yourself, little moth. But you've already changed." She pointed down to where the tree roots were wrapping around my ankles. "Your feet are rooted, soon your bones will know the shape of silence. The forest accepts you."

"I won't be kept!" I snapped. "Not by the forest, not by you, and I won't let you keep them, either!"

The spirit sighed, something between fondness and exasperation. "You think I am the warden."

She turned, slowly, gesturing to the hanging cocoons that lined the clearing. Dozens more now, strung between branches like glowing fruit. Some were tiny. Some writhed. Some wept tears of liquid silver.

"I was the first. A girl too curious. Too brave. I stepped off the path and into a story spun from silk and rot. They fed me poems, told me I was chosen, said I had become more than flesh. And when I bled enough to drown the sun, they called it holy."

Around us, the wind picked up, the clearing darkened, and as she spoke, her voice grew more agitated with each word.

"So I *became* the story. Became the cage. They speak my name in reverence, but it is not my name. They remember me as wings and grace, not the girl who screamed while they turned her into a myth."

With more confidence than I felt, I stepped forward. "If you hate what they did, why do you keep taking the girls?"

The spirit's wings flared, light flashing across their many panes. Her hands balled into fists, beads of blood dripping from where her nails dug too deep.

"I do not *take* them," she sneered at me. "I receive them. I am the box they lock their daughters in while they pretend they're setting them free."

Her gaze—Yara's eyes again—narrowed. "You came with your own wings. Made of glass and blood and choice. That has not happened in... centuries."

I touched the base of my wings, where copper wires met my spine. The cool metal grounded me as I took another step forward.

"I didn't come to be changed. I came to undo."

The spirit's many eyes slowly blinked. "Will you kill me, little moth?

"No." I stepped into the ring of mushrooms. "I'll break you open."

I ran. My heart threatened to beat out of my chest, but a wave of calmness steadied my stride. *I am not afraid.*

The cocoon pulsed as I reached it. Light flared, and the spirit screamed—not in rage, but in *warning*. The ground split beneath my feet. Roots shot up, twisting and grasping. My wings snapped outward, catching the air as I leapt, spun, and twisted away. Glass sliced bark as wires snagged against the surface.

I dove my hands into the silk of the cocoon.

Magic burned against my flesh. Visions slammed into my skull—girls crying, laughing, forgetting their names—a storm of *what might have been*. I shoved deeper, through heat and silk and memory, until my fingers scraped skin.

"Yara!" I called out in desperation. They would not have her, not when we were so close. I could not fail now. A single hand broke through and grasped mine. Hope, small and fragile, bloomed in my chest like the flutter of wings.

The cocoon burst—light and ash sweeping outward in a blinding wave. Around it, the ring of mushrooms erupted, spilling a cloud of black spores that stung the air. Trees howled as their branches bent and shuddered. The air itself cracked, sharp as breaking glass. I grew so dizzy I squeezed my eyes shut to keep the world from spinning.

When I opened my eyes, I was on my knees.

Yara lay beside me, dazed and blinking. Her silk wings were gone, the once beautiful gown torn asunder. Her skin was pale and covered in luminous bruises. With a strangled sob, she reached for me blindly, and I grasped her hands in mine, whispering words of comfort as I pressed my forehead against hers. Relief coursed through me as I held her in my arms, safe and alive. Yara was alive.

"You came for me!" She said between tears. Gently wiping them away, I laughed.

"You doubted that I would?" I helped her to stand, "I would go to the ends of the earth to find you, and even then, I wouldn't stop until we were together again. I love you, Yara."

"Not as much as I love you. You are the best thing to ever happen to me, Iris." She cried even harder. Throwing her arms around me, she pressed her lips to mine. I could taste the salt from her tears, or maybe it was mine. I couldn't tell where one ended and the other began. So, I leaned into her, desperate to make the moment last.

Across the clearing, the spirit stood on unsteady feet, her wings torn and her face fractured.

"You broke the spell," she said. Her voice was softer now, almost hollow. "The way is open." She lifted a shaking finger, pointing to somewhere behind us.

Yara and I spun around. A path had formed, light-filled and tranquil, with no illusions or loops. It led out of the woods, to home, to freedom, to anywhere we wanted to go. As the sun warmed our faces, I squeezed her hand in mine. Whatever direction we chose, we'd do it together.

I turned to the spirit. In another life, I could have been

her. As she began to fade, light bleeding from her seams, I gave her a nod of respect and gratitude.

"I was not meant to be eternal," she whispered. "Thank you for breaking me."

Then she was gone.

Only the wings remained, scattered like fallen stars across the forest floor.

12

TWO BUTTERFLIES EMERGING FROM A SHARED COCOON

BY CODY DRACO

It's become apparent to me
that both of us need to expand our vocabulary.
What's another word for sorry
when "love" is no longer qualified
to stand as a substitute for "you and me"?
As it has been watered down and commercialized
to the point of being something neither of us recognize.

We never thought we would "love" again,
but here we are, doing what accidental "lovers" do.
With each other's movements, we are so in tune
that it is no longer possible to read the room.

We both apologize excessively
for going about our business
and existing inconveniently.
We are overly considerate to a fault,
letting the world spin while it leaves us behind.

We slow dance together, out of step with time,

slipping into the warm bathtub rhythm innate to us
that others who hurriedly shower can't help but be confused
by.

They can look and laugh at us all they want,
but little do they know they will be silenced soon
by two butterflies emerging from a shared cocoon.

13

COCOON

BY KRISTEN ARGYRES

When a long day leaves me feeling
Not the windshield, but the bug
I inch along, right home to you

With one look, you see me reeling
Wrap me in a crushing hug
A safe, warm chrysalis for two

Your arms reshape my form anew
From a weary puddle of goo

You dry my tears so I might soar
And cast off my cocoon once more

14

HOW PENELOPE FOUND HER WINGS

BY CASIE BAZAY

Penelope chewed on her bottom lip as she pulled the toothpick from the center of the soufflé. It was nearly perfect. But not quite.

For the past five evenings, she'd baked the same dessert, and each day, there was a problem of some sort: Too overdone. Too sweet. Too lumpy. Didn't rise properly. And now, so close but still a tad soggy in the middle. If she put it back in the oven, she knew the edges would burn.

After trying a bite, Penelope scooped another spoonful and offered it to the feline perched on the adjacent barstool. Caterpillar sniffed, then delicately licked the proffered dessert before turning away.

"Ugh." Penelope sighed. Even Caterpillar didn't care for it. Or then again, maybe he was just sick of raspberry soufflé.

She covered the small white dish with saran wrap and placed it in the fridge. She'd probably finish it off later while watching the late evening news. Snacking helped with the depressing nature of it all. In the meantime, she planted herself on the barstool next to the one Caterpillar occupied and opened her monarch tracking app.

"Look here," she said to the cat, her spirits immediately lifting. "A kaleidoscope was spotted north of Oklahoma City earlier today." She patted her companion's head. "Hopefully, we can find them tomorrow."

Caterpillar responded by licking his right paw.

"Remember how they like to roost in those trees down near Pearson Creek? They have the last few years, anyway. But we'll check all the usual places in the morning."

Caterpillar moved on to licking his tail; Penelope was well aware that he desired a perfectly preened coat as much as she desired perfect desserts. And as much as she wanted to secure a spot for the monarchs on the Endangered Species list. It was truly the only way to save them.

Butterflies.

For as long as she could remember, Penelope had adored them. Some might say she was outright obsessed with them. No surprise, she had wanted to study entomology in college, but after her mother's death near the end of her freshman year, Penelope never quite got around to going back.

Now twenty-six, she had settled for waiting tables, moonlighting as a freelance writer (and she was rather proud of her blog, *The Chrysalis Chronicles*). But every fall, Penelope spent much of her spare time tracking the monarchs as a citizen scientist. For her, the butterflies symbolized all that was beautiful and right with the world (which wasn't much anymore, to be honest). But if they disappeared altogether? Well, she just didn't think she wanted to live in a world without the monarchs.

Penelope closed out of the app, grabbed her laptop, and began working on her next blog post: 'Eyespots: Functional or Just for Fun?' Caterpillar tried to crawl into her lap, but she promptly placed him back on his barstool. It seemed he always wanted attention most when she was writing.

For the next several hours, she blissfully disappeared into her work, finishing the blog just in time to watch the news. Every night, it was more of the same, but out of some sadistic sense of duty, she simply had to watch. She went to bed thinking about global warming and the ever-rising cost of living but stared at the butterfly tattoo on her forearm until better thoughts flitted their way in.

"Time to go," she told Caterpillar just as the sun peeked over the horizon the following morning. The cat meowed as she slipped the harness over his fluffy body and connected the leash to the ring up top. Penelope took one last drink of her hot chocolate, then out the door they went into the less-than-crisp early October morning.

Dew clung to the grass, and wispy fog hung over the buildings like a cozy blanket, or perhaps a shroud—Penelope couldn't decide which—as she and Caterpillar ventured down the sidewalk. She'd always liked early mornings, the freshness and solitude of the start of the day, before cars began to clog up the streets and people rushed about, oblivious to what remained of the natural world in the midst of the city.

It was a five-block walk to Pearson Park, and she and Caterpillar made good time. If the monarchs had roosted there overnight, they'd still be in the trees, maybe just starting to warm their wings in preparation for the next stretch of their flight.

The park's play equipment sat empty, blessedly childless, at this time of day. It wasn't that Penelope didn't like children; she just preferred to enjoy the reverence of nature without their squeals and chatter. When she entered the little trail that wove through the trees, a familiar awe settled over her, one that only a place like this could invoke.

Gaze glued to the treetops, Penelope walked, or maybe more accurately, was led by Caterpillar, through the woods. However, no signs of the orange and black-winged insects appeared.

"They're not here," Penelope announced, just in case Caterpillar was wondering. "Let's head down near the river."

The streets were livelier now as they walked six blocks east. Penelope checked her phone. Seven thirty-eight. Three hours until she needed to leave for the restaurant.

The river bank, with its fragrant mix of cedar and fir, was another likely roosting location, but Penelope found no signs of the butterflies there either. So she and Caterpillar returned to her apartment complex and hopped into her little blue hatchback with its colorful array of butterfly stickers affixed to the back window. Hope lingered; there were still a few more places to check.

Caterpillar sat shotgun, buckled into his kitty harness, but eagerly watched out the window. He'd long since gotten over his annoyance at being restricted while in the car. Penelope checked her tracking app again, searching for any more local sightings. No luck.

"Where are you hiding?" she wondered aloud.

By ten o'clock, she'd still found no trace of the butterflies and work beckoned. Disappointment tugged at her heart, but she took Caterpillar home and headed to Tandy's Steakhouse. She was eyeing yet another new shopping center under construction on the corner of Third and Indianapolis when a flitting pair of dark and delicate wings caught her attention. Penelope slammed on the brakes to avoid hitting the butterfly, but seconds later, she jolted forward. Her face smashed into the pluming airbag as someone hit her from behind.

"Oh my God!" she yelped. Horns blared all around as her heart fluttered. She pushed herself upright, taking stock of her limbs and then checking her face in the mirror. No blood. Nose still in the right location. She took several deep breaths. With trembling hands, she pushed open her door and stepped out into the street just as the other driver did the same. His maroon compact car appeared to be French kissing the bumper of her hatchback.

"Are you okay?" she asked the man, who wore a white button down tucked into tan slacks, along with a deep frown.

He donned thick, black-framed glasses, which he pushed up his nose as he stared at her. "Fine. You?"

Penelope looked at their cars mushed together, then back at the man. "I think I'm okay."

"What happened? Why did you brake so suddenly?"

She was surprised to find no trace of anger in his voice, only curiosity. Her cheeks warmed. "There was an animal in the way."

The man looked from one side of the street to the other. "A dog?"

"I'm not sure. I didn't get a good look at it." How could she explain to this stranger that she'd caused an accident for the sake of a lone butterfly? He'd no doubt think she was nuts. "I'm really sorry about this," she said, hoping he'd forget all about the animal.

He studied her face, maybe searching for some type of injury. Perhaps he'd seen her head slam into the air bag. Slowly, his frown melted away. "I'm glad you're okay. Could have been a lot worse, I suppose."

Cars poked along, and people gawked.

"Should we maybe move over to the parking lot?" Penelope asked.

"I don't think we should move the cars. The police will arrive soon. I called them right away."

"No, I meant us. I don't want to stand here in the street."

The man pushed up his glasses again. On the outside, he definitely had a Clark Kent vibe going on. Dark, wavy hair. Bright green eyes. Nice, sturdy shoulders. And he looked to be no more than thirty, at most.

"Sure," he agreed.

Penelope was glad he wasn't one of those angry, road rage types. He could be screaming at her right now, but instead, he seemed utterly calm. Gradually, her shakiness subsided.

Sirens wailed in the distance, and within a matter of seconds, the police arrived, taking both drivers' accounts of the accident, as well as their personal information. A wrecker hauled away their cars, which had clung to each other like long lost lovers for several awkward minutes.

It wasn't until all of this was over that Penelope realized she was late for work. "Oh fudge buckets," she exclaimed, pulling out her phone. She explained the situation to her manager, and Phil told her to take the day off.

"Were you heading to work?" Penelope asked the man, whom she'd since learned was named Mateo.

"No. I was actually on my way to a conference over at the Janson Center. I've got an Uber coming to get me now."

"What kind of conference?" Penelope asked.

"It's put on by the American Entomology Association each year. I'm a melittologist. I stud—"

"Bees," she cut in with a smile. She inspected Mateo with new interest.

One of his dark eyebrows lifted, then he returned the smile. "How did you know? Most people don't."

"I love insects. Butterflies, mostly, but I'm interested in all of them. I was going to study entomology in college, but I'm afraid I never finished."

"I see."

"It's terrible what's going on with the bees, isn't it?"

His smile faded, and he nodded. "Yes, quite." A white Hyundai pulled up beside them, and he reached for the door before glancing back at her. "It was nice to meet you, Penelope."

She'd never told him her name either, but he must have been paying attention when she spoke to the police as well. "Wait, is the conference free by chance? I would really love to attend."

Mateo paused, the car door ajar. "You actually had to register beforehand, but I believe I am allowed one guest. Would you care to join me?"

"I'd love to!"

As it turned out, Mateo was being modest when he said he was merely *attending* the conference; he was actually the featured speaker. Penelope was rapt as he so eloquently spoke about declining wild bee populations. Other speakers then took to the podium to educate attendees on their topics of specialty. It was all so fascinating, and Penelope could scarcely believe she was here with all of these professors, scientists, and fellow entomology enthusiasts.

However, she was equally thrilled when Mateo asked if she'd like to join him for an early dinner after the conference.

"Sure," she agreed. "I'd love to pick your brain some more. There is so much interesting information I wasn't aware of—"

Mateo laughed. “Okay, great.”

“This will be fun!” Penelope caught herself bouncing on the balls of her feet—something she couldn’t remember doing in a long, long time. After all, how often did she get the chance to talk with someone with interests so similar to her own? A short pause followed as Mateo seemed to survey her face again. Penelope cleared her throat. “So you’re from Tulsa? How do you like it there?”

“Oh, it’s fine. I grew up in Boston but ended up at Oklahoma State University for my masters, and well, I guess the state kind of grew on me, so I stuck around.” Their second Uber of the day arrived and Mateo opened the door to allow Penelope in first. “There’s a great steakhouse called Tandy’s I hear. Everything is locally sourced.”

“Actually, do you mind if we eat somewhere else? That’s where I work. Don’t get me wrong, they have amazing food, but my manager kind of gave me the day off after the wreck and it would just be weird to go in with a...”

“Date?” Mateo provided, offering up another smile.

“Uh, yes,” Penelope said, though she’d been about to refer to him as a friend. Apparently, he thought of this as more than just a couple of insect lovers chatting about their passion over a plate of food. Penelope wasn’t sure what to make of that but decided she’d rather go on a date with Mateo than not go to dinner with him at all.

“Totally understand,” he said. “What else do you suggest then?”

“How about The Water Front? It’s also locally sourced, and they have amazing appetizers.”

“The Water Front it is.”

Dinner wasn’t nearly as awkward as Penelope had anticipated. Mateo was chatty, even more so after half a glass of wine. She explained how she helped track the monarchs moving through central Oklahoma every fall and how, in fact, that was what she'd been out doing this very morning before the wreck.

"That's important work," Mateo said. "The butterflies. The bees. It's all connected. The global collapse of these pollinating communities is everyone's problem. Or, rather, it should be. Even though it's not on most people's radar at all. I just don't know how they can be so..." He waved a hand, appearing to search for the right word.

"Oblivious?" Penelope offered, the familiar outrage beginning to simmer beneath the surface of her skin.

He nodded. "I was going to say apathetic, but yes. It's like they're just continuing on with their lives as if everything is perfectly fine, driving their gas guzzling trucks and SUVs and eating all of their monoculture-farmed food without a care in the world. I don't understand it."

"Me either!"

Penelope had never met another person who cared so much about the things she did. In fact, she couldn't relate to most people her age at all. That was why she'd given up on dating and all of that stuff that other twenty-somethings cared so much about. In the past, when she did attempt to go out on a date, she'd inevitably start ranting about the environment or some related topic and their eyes would glaze over and things went downhill from there. Somehow, she didn't think that would happen with Mateo, but she vowed to control herself.

She took another sip of wine. "Mateo, I'm afraid I have to confess something."

"Oh? Is your other vehicle a monster truck?" He gave her a wry smile.

Penelope laughed. "No, I only have one car. But I wanted to tell you... it wasn't a dog."

"I'm sorry, I don't follow."

"The wreck. I didn't brake for a dog. It was a Swallowtail."

Mateo's lips pressed together for just an instant, but then a smile spilled out. "A Swallowtail? Is that so?"

Penelope smiled back, though she tapped her fingers nervously on her thighs.

He merely shrugged. "I don't blame you for omitting that detail. To tell the truth, I would brake for a bee. Well, if I could see it. I likely wouldn't. But I'm not angry. Actually, I'm rather glad I ran into you today. Literally!" He gave a joyful, boisterous laugh that Penelope decided she rather liked.

"You are?"

"Yes." He held up his glass for a toast. "To serendipitous car wrecks that spare the lives of butterflies."

They clinked glasses.

"I'm so glad you aren't mad about my fib."

"Not at all. I really like you, Penelope."

Warmth bloomed in her cheeks. Aside from being the friendliest and one of the smartest men she'd ever met, Mateo was also quite forward. But she could be too, she supposed. "I really like you too, Mateo."

His eyes twinkled as they seemed to share a moment of silent admiration for one another. "So what about dessert? Are you a fan?"

"Actually, I prefer to make my own. I would normally never ask this, but would you like to come back to my apartment for some raspberry soufflé? I've been working on perfecting it all week, and I have a feeling that tonight is the night."

"Soufflé, huh? Sounds enticing."

Back at her apartment, Mateo sat on the barstool beside

Caterpillar, and both gentlemen watched as Penelope whisked together the ingredients.

"So you love dessert and butterflies, and you work as a waitress and a writer. What else should I know about you, Penelope?" He reached over to stroke Caterpillar's head, which the cat allowed for now.

"Oh, lots probably, but I don't want to talk about myself. There's much more important stuff in the world. Like milkweed, for instance. We need a milkweed movement, wouldn't you agree?

Instead of HOAs regulating all of these dumb and, frankly, detrimental policies, they should start requiring something useful—like milkweed gardens. It wouldn't be difficult at all. And while I'm on the topic of difficult, why is it so mother trucking hard to get the monarchs onto the endangered species list? I just don't get it." Penelope realized she'd been waving her spatula around like a madwoman. She lowered her hand.

Mateo's eyes hadn't glazed over, but his forehead creased with a look of concern. "Penelope?"

"Yes?"

"It's okay. I get it. You care. A lot. And so do I. But it's okay to talk about other things, too. I know there's a lot wrong with the world, but if you really think about it, there's a lot of good in it, too."

"Such as what?"

"Us?"

"Us?" Penelope blinked stupidly.

"We have an unbelievable amount of common interests, haven't you noticed? I know we only just met, but I would love to see you again. If you would like that, anyway." He held up his hands. "No pressure, of course."

Here Mateo was, being all forward again. But this time,

the warmth skipped her cheeks and went right down to her heart.

"I would actually like that, too. But aren't you going back to Tulsa tomorrow?"

He sighed. "I've got to get the car situation figured out first, but it's only a two-hour drive. We could meet in the middle. Or I could come here. I don't mind."

"You'd drive all the way back here for me? What about the fuel?"

Caterpillar suddenly jumped into Mateo's lap where he proceeded to purr loudly. "I drive a hybrid, you know," Mateo said, stroking the cat's head again. "I mean, who knows what kind of loaner they'll give me, but it's okay."

Penelope put the soufflé dishes into the oven and turned back to face Mateo. "I think I'd like that very much." She couldn't believe she was saying this to a man she'd only met this morning. But Mateo wasn't just any man. He looked like Clark Kent and he was a melittologist, not to mention, quite possibly the most interesting person she'd ever met in her life. And maybe best of all, Caterpillar, who never warmed up to anyone quickly, was already giving his stamp of approval.

As the soufflés baked, Penelope poured them each another glass of Merlot and told Mateo about losing her mother when she was nineteen and how she'd never been the same since. But also, how getting Caterpillar had helped to heal her heart a little.

Mateo told her about his rescue mutt, Frisco, who loved to go for walks and chase tennis balls and shake hands.

"Caterpillar goes for walks, too. On a leash. He loves it."

Mateo looked down at the orange cat in his lap who was, once again, licking his paw. "You don't say?"

Penelope held her breath as she removed the twin

desserts and thought: *Please, creator of the universe, let them turn out perfect tonight.*

And as it so happens, they did.

The next morning, Penelope picked up Mateo at his hotel in her little red loaner car and they drove south in search of the monarchs. He'd mentioned the night before that he'd like to join her, and she and Caterpillar, who now sat just as attentively in the back seat, were glad to have his company.

"I always feel guilty about my carbon footprint while I'm trying to locate the monarchs, but I tell myself the importance of the work balances it all out, you know?"

"I would definitely agree." Mateo sipped his coffee. Penelope had brought along a small thermos full of hot chocolate, which she sipped from as well.

Half an hour later, Penelope took the highway exit toward Norman.

"The monarchs like OU?" Mateo teased. "I assumed they were Cowboy fans since they don my alma mater's colors and all."

Penelope laughed. She couldn't remember the last time another person made her laugh so much. Maybe it had been her mother. "They like the area around Lake Thunderbird. It's one of my usual check-in spots."

"Ah. Good to know."

They pulled into a campground, where they got out and wandered the area, Caterpillar leading the way, as usual.

"He's a funny cat," Mateo remarked.

"I just love how confident he is. He knows he's not like other cats, but I think he's rather proud of that." Penelope gazed fondly at her feline friend. "I really aspire to be more like Caterpillar."

"Maybe Caterpillar learned his ways from you."

"You think so?" Penelope smiled, something good and pure filling up the empty space in her chest, the one she hadn't thought much about until now. "Maybe so." Just then, something caught her eye, over near the lake shore. Her heart soared. "Oh my word, look! There they are!"

Mateo followed her gaze. "Amazing!"

They stopped in their tracks and stared. Caterpillar tugged at his leash, but after a moment, gave up and sat on his haunches. Penelope pulled out her phone and snapped as many photos as she could. The kaleidoscope continued south over the lake, one big fluttering mass of orange and black and beauty. Penelope surmised there were at least a hundred of them, if not more. She couldn't believe it.

"This group seems slightly larger than the one I saw last year," she noted. Her face broadened in a wide smile.

"That's good news."

"I'd say so." By the time the monarchs disappeared from sight, tears shone in her eyes. Mateo didn't comment, but she felt the need to explain anyway. "They just bring me so much joy, actually seeing them in person. As a kid, I think I took them for granted, but now, it's just so rare. It feels really special, you know?"

"I get it, Penelope. I really do." He took her hand in his, smiling gently. "Is this okay?"

His hand was warm and perfectly cocooned her own. A shiver coursed through her body. "It's more than okay."

As they walked back to the car, Penelope's heart seemed to gain monarch wings of its own.

She realized Mateo was right. There was still an awful lot of good in the world, too.

15

PAPILLON NOIR

BY MICKEY BLACK

Butterfly kisses on gooseflesh,
Your taste, salty on my lips.
Hearts flutter in rhythmic palpitations,
There's magic in your fingertips.

At last, we fall together,
My stomach, full of butterflies.
An eternity I've longed to be,
Lust's source, gleaming in your eyes.

"Butterfly," you called me,
That night our souls aligned.
A metamorphosis of passion,
Our love is so divine.

16

AN EMAIL NEVER SENT

BY BRI EBERHART

from: melanielovesbutterfly11@gmail.com
to: hd141@gmail.com
date: Jun 6, 2025, 4:43 PM
subject: (no subject)
mailed-by: Draft

Dear Harry,

I'm unsure if this will make its way to you. I've started and backspaced... a lot. But there are some things I need to get off my chest. So, maybe I'll be brave enough to hit send when I'm finished.

Do you remember our senior year? How our lives were already planned, and everything was still ahead of us? Our hopes, our dreams, our future?

After our high school graduation ceremony, we planned to meet at the boardwalk. We didn't want to celebrate with anyone else.

It was only supposed to be you and me, as always.

But then you never came.

I sat there, watching the merry-go-round spin for hours. The repetitive chime of the organ suffocated me as I wondered where you were. The sweet tang of cotton candy in the air flipped my stomach as I tried to swallow the truth —dazzling lights fractured by tears blurring my vision.

After picking myself up off the bench, I made my way back toward reality. My red Honda Civic sat alone in the parking lot, and I laughed.

If I didn't laugh, I would've cried.

I drove home, all the while thinking, you should have been there.

How could plans crumble so easily? How could the past four years mean so little to you? I needed to know, yet I couldn't bring myself to ask.

You left me a letter apologizing before leaving for a different college. A school we didn't plan for—and with that, the shocking revelation that this had been a long time coming. You planned for this. And yet, I was only an afterthought.

I was worth a proper goodbye.

Do you remember our first real date? It was the Homecoming dance our freshman year. The shy smile you gave me in the hallway as you leaned your back against my locker.

Your voice shook when you asked me out, and to be honest, that's what won me over. Of course, I had had a crush on you for a while at that point, but that's neither here nor there.

I was thrilled to be your Homecoming date. I remember thinking, *the scribblings in my notebook must've paid off.*

Friends helped find me a new dress before the big night —red, floor-length, with lace on the top. They helped me curl my hair and topped it off with a gold butterfly clip to pin back one side. Did you know that night was the first time I ever wore lipstick?

I had no idea what I was doing.

But you didn't either. And that was nice.

I wasn't alone.

~

Do you remember when you moved here? Do you remember health class in middle school when we were paired together your first week in town?

My cheeks flamed as you sat down next to me, introducing yourself. You held out your hand, and I was so worried my palm would be sweaty. I rubbed my hands on my pants underneath the table, just in case.

But I think you were nervous, too. Of course, I didn't know that. But I've learned a lot about your facial expressions since then. I can read you like a book after all the years we've spent together. Or at least, I thought I could. Still, as it all comes back to me now, the memory of your wide eyes and slight smile fills me with gratitude.

We might've always been on the same page—until now.

~

Our story helps rewind time. It brings me back to when I was young and naive, with so much affection to give.

But maybe I didn't know what love was back then. How could I?

Maybe we were always two ships passing in the night. You were what I needed then. And I hope I was what you needed, too.

Some things aren't meant to last forever.

The only thing that still haunts me is how it ended.

How you were there one day and gone the next.

I was worth a proper goodbye.

WELL... I guess that's all I wanted to say. Sorry if this is a bit awkward, but it'll probably sit in my drafts anyway. I thought it would make me feel better, but to be honest, I don't think anything has changed.

Maybe that's because I know you haven't read this yet. The cursor's never-ending blink is still sitting on my screen, taunting me with each passing second. But even if you do receive this, will you only hit delete?

My finger hovers over the mouse, and I count my breaths until I dare to hit send. I add one more note:

If you do see this, I hope you're well. I hope life is good.

Don't mind me.

I'll be fine—just like the butterfly, I'll find my new beginning.

—Melanie

17

LOSE YOU IN A BLINK

BY LAURA JORDAN

When I close my eyes, I can't catch you. You change into colors blending, shapes morphing, a work of abstract art I can't pin down.

My mind's eye—blind, but it never scared me. How I can't picture objects, places. People. Until I had you, and I didn't want to lose you in a long blink. Forget your face covered in oatmeal. The way your hair stands on end when you first wake. Close my eyes too long, and you're a phantom just out of reach.

Like chasing butterflies.

The way you did those summer days running over the grassy hills. Through giant sprinklers that glittered rainbows in the sky, outmatched only by your boundless giggles. Where scents of sunscreen and cracker crumbles mixed with the heat of your tiny body pressed to mine, and I carried you back to the car. Drove home for naptime.

But I feel you. This kaleidoscope version of you twisting in my mind. Every melting popsicle, chattering squirrel, afternoon rain. Every flutter of a butterfly's wings returns you to me.

You'll always be my little one chasing butterflies.

18

PERSPECTIVE OF A FALLING LEAF

BY ABIGAIL DAVIS

Floating, drifting, closer to the Earth.
In a few moments, I will settle in, joining
my brothers and sisters—a quiet embrace upon nature's carpet.
Soon after, I will disappear into the soil, becoming
nutrients for this very tree I have called my home
for many dances between the sun and moon.

I rest now.
Looking back up to where I once hung;
I miss the view of being above everything.
I watched the children playing
in the park, the summer sun tanning
their skin—the same sun that warmed my cells
and coaxed me to grow back in Spring
when the bird's nest was built two branches over.
I saw those baby birds take their first flights.
One day they never returned; the nest sits empty now.
At least, in my memory it will always remain so.

A child picks me up to admire my colors.
She smiles, delicately tracing my edge
with her tiny finger, then quickly drops me.
A brief moment soon to be filtered from her mind;
nonetheless, I am grateful for it.

I was never meant to last.
My surface dried until I could crumble at the lightest touch.
My once vibrant green was drained from me.
In its place: a deepened purple and red,
with a spot of brown on my edge
from where I provided a meal to a caterpillar, nourishing
its small form so it could change shape.

If I could alter one thing about my short existence,
it would be this: I would have been a butterfly;
beautiful, and free, and flying.

Yet, even in my absence of wings,
I will treasure the one flight I was granted.

19

BLOOMED FLOWERS

BY TRINITY PIERCE

A flower, its petals dyed in pinks and purples, swayed gently in the warm breeze. The sun was a white, boiling ball hanging overhead. The flower couldn't shake off the sense of unease and discomfort that filled its stem and rattled its leaves; the feeling weakened when a butterfly fluttered past, its wings a vibrant, soda-candy blue that faded to a deep brown at the edges. It danced around the flower, but didn't flit close enough to touch it.

It's quiet, the flower thought. To its surprise, it could think. It felt nice to think, to wonder. The flower decided to do it again. *And how exceedingly strange that I am growing here.* A thinking being deserved a name, and it only took a swift glance at its petals to settle on one: Carnation, or Carnie for short.

Carnie couldn't help but feel a twinge of disappointment. The flower could have sprouted in a palace garden, an old woman's front yard, or a meadow. Instead, Carnie blossomed in the middle of the street.

It wasn't even a nice road: cracks spread across its

surface like silk in a spider's web. In fact, the whole place looked rather awful. Vines and greenery snaked through dilapidated houses lining the road. The butterfly hovered near a rusty billboard with a peeling poster of a beaming, dark-eyed man holding a smiling, blond-haired woman, the words, *HOLD ME TIGHT: COMING THIS SUMMER,* written in big, block letters. The metal skeleton of an abandoned playground loomed to Carnie's right, and a swing creaked every time the wind whistled through its rusting chain. Something like black chalk marked shapes onto a wall nearby, but Carnie couldn't see the exact drawings scrawled on it.

Graffiti, trash, and weeds growing freely, Carnie scoffed. *Not just a bad road, but a bad neighborhood by the looks of it.*

Carnie's pride stung from the blow. Surely it was worth more than a commonplace dandelion or clover. A *carnation* deserved to be looked at, admired, loved. Yet here Carnie bloomed. Even the butterfly wouldn't touch it.

How unbecoming. If Martha knew of this—

Martha? A name, an unknown name. Carnie strained against its roots, curving its long neck until the flower nearly kissed the asphalt. There must be a reason for the name. The butterfly alighted on a nearby post, folding its wings neatly behind itself. Straightening its stem, Carnie concentrated every fiber of its being on the name. Martha. M. A. R. T. H. A.

Nothing.

The creak of the swing continued, like a metronome. Like a song. The sound of soft, sweet humming joined it as a bee lazily drifted by the flower, fully gorged on nectar. Carnie hummed along with it.

Sweet flower moon,
bless me with your glow,

make each star a diamond,
so I may give them all to her,
oh, our love will bloom,
if you will shine...

Moonlight, by Gene Benedict.

Perhaps the name Martha was from the song, and Carnie had heard the song as a seedling.

The heat of the sun burned into the flower's delicate body with renewed intensity. Apprehension pulled at its petals. Just when Carnie was sure they would pop off, the butterfly flew past it, its wings barely brushing the tips of the flower's petals. Carnie shot a whisper of thanks, but the butterfly kept going until it glided out of sight, and nothing remained except the squeak of the lone swing.

Silence, once peaceful, now seemed rather oppressive to Carnie. It lingered past its welcome, as if trying to lull the flower into a false sense of peace before snapping shut like a Venus flytrap. Carnie focused and fluttered its petals in defiance, breaking the silence, although only for a moment. Once the rustling subsided, silence returned.

The swing assisted in the battle against silence, which Carnie duly appreciated, though it missed the butterfly and wished the insect would return.

Then, a creature crested the horizon.

The thing scrambled up the road on all fours. Filthy rags hung off of its skeletal frame, and as it approached Carnie, the flower was shocked to discover that it was a human child. Dirt and grime caked the child's face, and when they noticed Carnie, a set of happy shrieks and noises erupted from it. Their mouth widened into a gap-toothed grin. The child crept up to the flower, which tried to straighten itself up.

Now, you listen here, you rascal. I understand you may want to pick a flower beautiful and perfect like I, but my place is not in whichever of these shacks you call a home. Carnie fluttered its petals disdainfully. *You see, I—*

The child couldn't seem to hear the flower; they reached their hand out. Carnie froze. The sun burned.

"Boy!"

The child turned and looked back at the road. Over the crest came another human. Dirty, greasy locks draped across the person's shoulders, and their bones jutted out like thorns, sharp and ready to pierce. An animal carcass was slung over their shoulder, and they walked with a limp. This one didn't seem quite as abysmal as the child, but they certainly weren't in a good state, either.

"How many times do I need to tell you, stick close 'fore you get hurt or worse," the person—a woman—said.

The half-feral boy's grin turned into an arch. "Yes, Mama," he said. He looked at Carnie, and his face brightened again. "But, Mama, lookie here at this!"

The woman limped over, the corners of her mouth tilting upward. "A flow—" she began, then trailed off. As quickly as it came, the smile disappeared. The woman's face drained of color and she stopped, looking at the spot behind Carnie.

"Acklewood Street," she muttered. "I forgot we were on Acklewood Street."

Carnie and the boy looked at the woman, both tilting their heads (or in Carnie's case, its petals).

The woman rubbed her shoulders. "All right, Sammy, let's keep movin'."

Sammy took a step, then hesitated, looking at Carnie. The boy's eyes lit up, and the flower slouched as his stubby fingers wrapped around its stem and pulled.

Carnie's chance to be appreciated by someone worthy,

stolen. Deep down, the flower wondered if that had ever been possible. Carnie tried to cheer itself up. *Well, at least I can see what all the fuss was about.*

The flower's stem drooped. The thing that had made the woman go quiet was nothing more than a heap of faded clothes with some bleached bones sticking out of it. *Roadkill.* Carnie attempted to reassure itself: at the very least, it would soon be out of this dump.

"Mama, I gotchu a gift," the boy said, beaming proudly, the flower clutched in one grimy, outstretched hand.

The woman looked at the boy for a moment, then smiled. "Thank you, Sammy," she said, and took the flower.

Her hands were rough, but surprisingly, Carnie's unease faded, replaced with a comforting warmth. The woman lifted the flower to her face. Her lips were cracked, her gums bleeding, and her remaining teeth blackened. Cheekbones protruded as though carved from alabaster. Her eyes were a deep blue, like sapphires, or the sky before dawn cracked through its delicate veneer. Shiny jewels, with a glaze of... tears?

Martha.

There it was, the name again, rising up like a sprout pushing through soil, like a mole clawing for the surface. But right before it broke through, the name disappeared.

"It can sit right here," the woman said, tucking the flower into her worn hat. "How's it look?"

The boy clapped excitedly. "It's really pretty!"

Electricity jolted through Carnie's leaves. *At least even a creature like that can recognize beauty.*

The woman, the flower, and the boy moved on for some time. The street seemed to stretch on infinitely, a black snake threading between the crumbling houses. There were more shapes on the walls, some clustered together. The outline of a boy and a girl playing tag. A man sitting on a bench. A woman walking her dog.

A sick, twisted ache crawled up the flower's stem. Carnie was sure it would wilt and die if it looked at the outlines for too long, so the flower drooped its head slightly.

Then, they came to the top of a hill, and the ache strengthened to a stab. The neighborhood stretched out to a ruined and decayed city, a patchwork of twisted metal and contorted wreckage. Ugliest of all were the craters that pockmarked the ground, like holes left by earthworms after a heavy rain. Carnie burned so hot, the flower feared it would disintegrate. Leaves, stem, and petals: it would all meld together into one unrecognizable lump of burnt refuse. The rays of the sun offered no mercy. A flash of something painful, something treading the edge of a memory and a dream, made Carnie shiver.

A hint of blue and brown appeared at the edge of Carnie's vision. The flower twisted itself as much as it could, but the butterfly was gone as quickly as it had come.

After traipsing through the seared, blistered suburbs, they eventually stood in front of a house on the outskirts of the city. Carnie grudgingly admitted that although the house was blackened and had some busted windows, it wasn't too bad. Greyed lace curtains framed the empty sills, and peeled blue paint still clung to sections of the exterior. The boy ran to the yard, grabbed a deflated ball, and kicked it about.

The woman heaved open the garage door, then threw the carcass onto a bloodstained table. Carnie tried to focus on the moldy ceiling while the woman worked. When the woman finished, she tossed the skin over a rack and picked up the meat.

"Sammy," she yelled as she walked to the front door, "get over here. Grab me something for your gift."

Sammy gave the ball one last hard kick before running to the door, ducking under the woman's arm, and racing into the house.

Carnie was soon transferred into a metal pot, though there was scarcely enough water to cover the bottom. Nothing could survive for long with so little water. Carnie trembled. Martha was still a mystery, and the flower couldn't fade without an answer.

Carnie managed to quit shaking as the woman and Sammy set about with their chores. The boy chopped herbs, while the woman sliced meat.

An hour later, the woman lay curled up on a ragged couch. Sammy rested on a soiled mattress next to her, lazily gnawing on a bone. The woman's eyelids started to drift shut, but popped back open when the boy spoke.

"Mama," he said, "won't you sing to me?"

"Sammy, it's been a long day and I'm tired," the woman muttered. "It's time to rest."

"Please Mama, pleaseee?" Sammy begged. "I got you a flower and everything!"

"First of all, gifts aren't s'posed to cost anything," the woman grumbled. "But since you helped catch something today, I'll let it slide."

The boy smiled contentedly and closed his eyes.

The song drifted out, smoothly, cleanly,

"Sweet flower moon..."

The butterfly flew in through the open window, landing on the edge of the pot. Its black eyes glistened in the moonlight. Carnie and the butterfly listened to the woman's song, and neither moved an inch.

Sammy snored. "Y'know, that was my mama's favorite

song," the woman whispered. She bit her lip, stroking the boy's hair. "Before I was grown up, back when I was still just 'lil Jenny, she'd hum it to me 'fore I slept. Daddy always said no one else was born to be a singer like Martha Blackwell." A tear slid down her cheek. "I should've known he'd have tried to go back for her, even in the middle of all that hell. Mama wasn't kidding when she said Daddy would always find his way back to her."

The butterfly flapped its wings, and Carnie understood right then who Martha was.

You'll have to forgive me. You know I've always been slow on the uptake.

The butterfly twitched an antenna, then flew out the window.

The next day, Jenny and Sammy left. One benefit of the pot was that Carnie could move around freely, unfettered by roots and soil. The butterfly eventually returned, and together they watched as the woman brought back a bundle of clothes and bones, clung to each other as Jenny and the boy dug a hole, and soaked in the peaceful quiet when they huddled around it.

She's so big now. But she's still our Jenny. She looks just like you.

The butterfly carefully crawled onto the flower's petals, and they sat together for a while.

"Mama, look! A butterfly," Sammy said, running to the window.

The woman's eyes crinkled. "A blue butterfly. Mama came to visit, like she promised."

Orange rays blanketed the house in a warm light, and this time, the sun didn't burn. Carnie basked in the heat, and though it was only a matter of days before its petals wilted and its stem sagged, there was an air of calm about the flower.

Death scared me, darling, but it paled in comparison to losing you.

The butterfly's wings quivered, and Carnie caressed the butterfly with a velvet petal. Their second chance didn't go to waste: they enjoyed the slice of heaven Jenny had grown amidst hell, and the butterfly stayed with Carnie right to the end.

20

BECOMING

BY ALANA AVELLINO

Where I began was a place of loneliness,
created out of ordinary circumstances,
but meant for beauty.
Magic existed at arm's length.
On the other side of life existed my oasis.
Quiet and determined, I endured a climb—
insignificant at times, monumental at others.
Never giving up, never giving in,
when the smallness begged.
Listening to the call of what is meant to be.
Destiny is inevitable and cannot be ignored,
even when it feels too big.

Crawling the Earth's floor for my freedom,
dreams of wings so beautiful and light,
I found safety.
A quiet place to rest my wandering soul.
A cocoon to look within, go within, feel within.
Shut out the world, retreat into darkness.
Find my heart and listen.

Wrap my weary body within the arms of myself,
within the arms of love.
Nurture and grow.
Metamorphosis is not graceful,
but it is becoming.

A space of limbo—
an in-between, before, and after solitude.
Strength becomes infinite, powerful, and
unveiling.
My reflection is different, brilliant, and
radiating.
Disarming, yet welcoming.
I am new, yet I am still me.
I never felt safe to fly.
Trust overpowers fear, faith overpowers
weakness.
I spread my wings.
Delicate and strong, born in the dark.
And soar.

21

THINGS WITH FEATHERS

BY E. H. PERRY

"Hope is the thing with feathers,"
That's what Emily said,
But I think Anxiety is
The thing with feathers instead.

A giant ash-gray bird
With a voice that rings like a gong,
It perches deep inside my gut,
And shouts, "Wrong, wrong, wrong."

So how could Hope also be
A thing with feathers too?
Then I learned about butterflies,
And I think Emily knew

That the bright tiny scales which
Grace a butterfly's wings,
Capture the air as it flies—
So they too are feathered things.

Sometimes Hope doesn't look
Like what you expect to find,
And instead of wings you see
Something of a different kind.

A small fuzzy worm that crawls
Away from the bird's attack,
And it looks like Hope will be
Anxiety's morning snack.

The angry bird pecks the worm,
Until it curls up and dies—
Or so it seems, but then—
It spreads its wings and flies.

Because Hope is a butterfly—
That can be hard to see
But when it seems all is lost,
It conquers Anxiety.

22

FLYING FREE

BY DESIRAE GRACYN

Shocking people is my jam, especially when a lot of them underestimate me. They like to tell me I'll never amount to anything or succeed. So, I enjoy proving them wrong. Seeing that dumbstruck look on their face, the one where their jaw hits the floor and their eyes threaten to fall out, excites me just a little too much.

As I rock on the comfy bench on my patio, the hot summer sun warming my bare shoulders, I recall the last time someone doubted my ability to finish a work project on time. I completed it with a week to spare.

I typically surprise people over the mundane everyday stuff. It's easy for me. I just wish I could do it with adventurous things, too. But I happen to avoid risks like the plague.

The back door creaks open, and a cold gush of air sways my black locks around my shoulders. Yasmin's floral perfume floats past me. With my elbow pressed on the bench's armrest, I turn to face her. She leans against the brick wall, her arms crossed, shaking her head. Her gorgeous rose pixie lines her face and accentuates her cheekbones.

"Lila, you really think you can do this?" Yasmin moves to stand in front of me. Her orange sundress's cotton hem brushes against my knees as she holds her hand out for my list.

"No. But I have to. I need to prove to myself I can." I write the last item on my adventurous checklist. *#5 Skydive.*

After another relationship failed due to my last girlfriend saying I couldn't be audacious, I realized things needed to change.

It's about time risky and adventurous tasks get crossed off my shock factor list. But for once, it isn't just about seeing others' surprised faces. This is about shocking *me.* I need to do this for myself. I can't always be so tightly wound by my anxiety.

I need to break free.

I hand Yasmin the list, my fingers graze against hers, and butterflies dance in my stomach. For years, she has been my best friend, but ever since my last relationship ended in shambles and I saw a new side of Yas as she helped me out of the mess, I've wanted more.

"This list is crazy!" She shakes the paper, and it rustles in the wind. "Number three: say yes for an entire day. Number four: hike the Grand Canyon. And..." she stutters. "Number five: jump out of a plane. These things are wild. The polar opposite of you."

"Exactly! That's the point." I stare into her sapphire eyes and fidget with my butterfly ring. She's never approved of me doing this. She is just as afraid of taking risks as me.

"When do you plan on doing this?" She arches her eyebrows and leans against the patio table behind her.

"Well..." I draw imaginary eights in the air with the toe of my boot. "I jump in four hours."

"No." She shakes her head. "You could die! Aren't you afraid?"

"Nope." I gulp. I most certainly am afraid, but I'm not going to admit it. That will give her more ammunition to convince me not to go through with this.

"Don't lie to me." She places her calloused hand on my shoulder, and my skin warms. "Please, don't do this."

"I'm sorry." I glide away from her and toward the house. With my forehead on the cold window pane, I peek at her from the corner of my eye. "I'm going to send you the address. I'd love for you to be there, but if you don't come, I'll understand."

"I'm not supporting you or this." She crumbles my list.

Shoulders slumped, I sigh and head inside. It hurts not to have her there. But I have to do this. If I know her like I believe I do, she'll show. She has to.

DRESSED in the most irritating tight jumpsuit, I lean against the wall next to the facility's opening. A massive field encompasses my left side. Jets take off from one of the two sections, and skydivers land on the other. On my right is the warehouse. Instructors teach several groups in one corner. In another area nearest me, people pose for pictures. Right by the front entrance stands a huge counter where jumpers sign up. I watch that spot with such intensity, my eyes might fall out. But I can't miss Yas. Any second, she'll walk through those sliding glass doors.

"The plane is about to leave. This is the third one you've passed up." The skydiving instructor holds a clipboard. His glasses slide down his nose as he stares at me with scrutinizing eyes.

Sweat drips down my neck. I can't go without seeing Yas, or at least ensuring everything is okay between us. "I'll take the next one."

"It's the last, so you better hope so. You already paid." His pen makes a loud, screeching sound on the board as he probably scratches out my name... again. "People," he mutters, then walks away.

I pull out my phone to a picture of Yasmine and me dressed for the Christmas gala last year.

We had to attend the event representing our spirit animals. With Yas's unfounded wisdom, she connects with the owl. She wore big oval golden glasses, a leather black dress, and a fur hat with an owl-feathered train that flowed around her shoulders. My spirit animal is the hedgehog, for overcoming obstacles. But ever since I started this journey of trying to free myself from my own inner hurdles, I've connected with the butterfly, so I dressed as such.

While I'm staring at the photo, my phone buzzes with an in-coming call. Yasmin's face appears on the screen.

"Hey!" I say a little too cheerfully.

"Have you jumped?" Urgency coats her words.

"Not yet." I fidget with the ring and stare at the newest group that enters the photo area. All of them smile and laugh. They look so free. So happy.

"You don't have to prove anything to your exes. They didn't deserve you, Lila. You're perfect just the way you are." She sniffles.

Tears fill my eyes. It's times like these when I think she might have feelings for me, too. Feelings I might destroy if I jump. I close my eyes and take a deep breath. "Look, Yas, this isn't because of them—"

"How is it not?" she screams into the phone, and I pull it away from my ear. "This whole wanting to break free happened after Karla broke up with you last winter."

"Karla helped me see that I let my fear control my life." I slide down the concrete wall. My hand not holding the phone shivers against the cold ground. "Have you ever wondered why I like shocking people? If I can do better than they suspect, keep surprising them, I'll never worry about losing my job. I live by my anxiety. I know it'll probably always be there, but I want to be in control of it. I want my creative, fun spirit to break free. Jumping out of a plane is a strong way to tell my anxiety that it's not in control anymore."

"Can't you do that some other way?" she groans.

Can I? I stare at the jumpers landing on the freshly mowed grass, the joy shining on their faces, and the people near the wooden fence clapping. I want that. "Yeah. I can. But I've decided to do this. It's a great way to show I'm flying free. Accepting the anxiety but not letting it run my life. I will be adventurous. I will take some risks. And most of all, I'm bringing back my fun side."

"Lila..." she draws out my name. I imagine her tugging at her hair. Her usual go-to thing when frustrated.

At this point, nothing I say will make her happy. "I have to go, Yas. I'm doing this." I hang up the phone and cradle my head between my knees.

Despite my being in love with her, she is my best friend. Aren't best friends supposed to be there no matter what? I wish she'd support me. She doesn't have to jump, but her being at the fence cheering me on would be nice.

My chest tightens, and my throat closes. A panic attack is seconds from igniting. I can hardly breathe. *Why am I doing this?* Yas is right. I shouldn't take this risk. But...

It gets harder to breathe, the cement walls closing in on me. I pull at my hair, taking on Yas's habit. My hair feels soft. My eyes widen. The sense test.

One thing I can feel: the itchy uniform.

One thing I can taste: my dry mouth.

One thing I can hear: instructors teaching the jumpers how to pull the chute.

One thing I can smell: the sunflowers and tulips bordering the warehouse.

One thing I can see: I lift my head. A slideshow flashes on the wall in front of me, displaying pictures of those who previously jumped.

Slowly, my lungs expand, and my chest stops feeling like it's crushing me. My breath returns to normal. I can do this. I stand, repocket my phone, zip up the suit, and stare outside, waiting for the instructor to come back for me.

About five minutes later, he appears, his bushy silver eyebrows arched. "You ready?"

"Yeah. I think so."

"All right." He bows his head to me and leads the way to the Twin Otters.

The plane looks old, rustic even. *Can it really hold all of us jumpers?*

Sweat starts to coat the back of my shirt. My steps slow so much, I'm practically tiptoeing. The instructor is now at least ten feet ahead of me and a foot away from the plane. He turns back around, shaking his head.

Come on, Lila, move! You're in control of your fear. I take another normal-sized step forward.

"Wait!" Yasmin yells.

I jump and whirl around. My braids slap my face. She showed. "Yasmin?"

She runs toward me while the instructors yell at her to

stay back. I rush after her, so they'll stop shouting and she won't get in trouble.

"I made it," she says, out of breath. "If you feel like this is something you have to do, I'll support you. I need you to know that." She speaks loudly to be overheard by the Twin Otters' noisy engine and propellers.

My eyes turn glassy. "Thank you."

"I also brought you something." She digs through her satchel.

"Are you coming?" the instructor calls.

I crane my neck to look at him. "One second, please." I face Yas again. "Hurry up."

Keys jingle in her bag, glass clinks, and papers crunch. She removes her hand after a few more seconds. It's clenched in a fist, hiding her gift.

"Even if your spirit animal is a hedgehog, you're my butterfly. You give me hope, you show me courage, and you're so full of passion. It's contagious." She laughs and unzips my suit just a smidge.

My breath hitches. Suddenly, the instructor disappears, the warehouse behind Yas vanishes, and it's just us in our own glorious bubble.

She gulps, grabs my tank top's strap, and pins a red butterfly to the shirt. "It's right next to your heart, so if your anxiety tries to defeat you up there, place your hand on the butterfly and know I am with you. You can do this."

Tears cascade down my cheeks like a river. "Yas."

"You can thank me later. I think your instructor is going to pop a blood vessel." She gestures to him.

I don't look. I just want to stare at her. "But..."

"Go. Fly. Prove to yourself that you're in control! This is your life, not anxiety's, not anyone else's. Go be my adventurous butterfly."

Wait, did Yas just call me her butterfly? Okay, she and I definitely have a lot to talk about after this. I better not die.

I give her a tight hug and rush back to the instructor.

He shakes his head. "Two seconds longer, I would've left you."

I don't doubt it. I shuffle behind him, rubbing the spot where the butterfly lapel pin rests.

We hop into the Twin Otters and squish next to five other jumpers and their tandems.

As we reach the right altitude, they won't stop talking about how exhilarating this is. I want to join the conversation, but I'm having a hard time not letting my anxiety take over.

"Is this your first time?" a girl, younger than twenty, with freckled cheeks, asks.

I nod, sweat beading down my neck and my knuckles turning white from my grip on the seat. Those next to me seem like they're practically on top of me, suffocating me, even though they aren't close to touching me.

"Same. My dad is the professional and my tandem partner. He does this all the time." She smiles at her dad, who has a scruffy beard and tattoos running down his neck.

He winks. "It's safe. Promise!"

The girl squeezes my hand, her touch gentle.

The first pair jumps into the clouds, and my heart lodges in my throat. I scoot my back against the plane's metal wall.

"You're okay," the girl reassures me as another pair jumps.

I can't believe I thought I could do this. Jump out of a moving vehicle to my death. My parachute might not open. It could malfunction.

Again, another pair jumps with their arms spread wide, embracing the open void.

Only two more groups before me.

The next duo jumps.

Nope. I can't do this. I'll stay on the plane. That won't be wrong, just cowardice.

The girl turns to me. "You made it this far. You can go all the way!"

Her dad buckles himself to her, and they step off the plane's ledge, gone in a flash.

My throat squeezes shut. I can't do this.

My tandem partner holds his hand out to me.

I shake my head, squeezing myself into the corner.

"Be courageous!"

My eyes widen, and I touch the butterfly pin. The same words Yas spoke.

I'm supposed to be courageous and take control of this fear. My anxiety needs to stop keeping my awesomeness caged in. It's time I unleash myself from this bondage.

I grasp his hand. He smiles and buckles me to him.

"Step off," he says as we reach the ledge of the plane, the cold air kissing my cheeks.

Taking a deep breath, I leap.

The wind takes hold of us. And it's the most freeing I've ever felt.

As I stare at the beautiful world beneath me, the white clouds beside me, and open my arms like their wings, my anxiety vanishes, and joy replaces it. My spirit soars.

I'm a butterfly, and I am flying free!

23

CHASING BUTTERFLIES

BY KENDRA ANN KEPLINGER

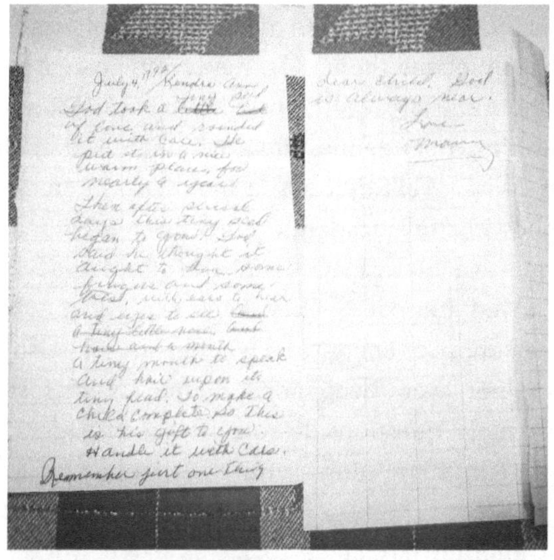

July 4, [illegible] Kendra Ann

God took a ~~little~~ tiny seed of love and rounded it with care. He put it in a nice warm place for nearly [illegible]

Then after several days this tiny seed began to grow. God said he thought it alright to give some fingers and some toes, with ears to hear and eyes to see ~~and a tiny little nose and hair and a mouth~~ a tiny mouth to speak and hair upon its tiny head. To make a child complete. So this is his gift to you. Handle it with care. Remember just one thing dear child, God is always near.

Love
Mommy

The last day of school always carried a strange magic-part goodbye, part relief, and whispers of what once was. Kori glanced over her "end- of-the- year" checklist and marked off "label classroom furniture with name and room number". The final thing standing between her and summer break was a signature from the vice principal—a task no simpler than a live action game of "Where's Waldo?", especially with several other teachers embarked on the same expedition. Kori checked her phone. Eleven a.m. She might as well rest a bit before aimlessly wandering the halls again. If only her mind could do the same.

How did she end up back here? Kori had sat in the same classroom when she was in the 7th grade and even remembered her seat. Three rows from the right. Second from the last desk. The best part? Witnessing the sheer terror of the students who currently sat in that desk when she shared the fact with her classes. Maybe they feared they'd become cursed as the next generation of middle school teachers. She didn't exactly blame them. Kori never anticipated returning to the school she swore she wouldn't go back to. Small town opportunities, a pandemic, and a national teacher shortage said otherwise. Well, that and a mountain of student debt from following the academic guidelines provided to the millennials to achieve a successful and affordable life.

She loved her kids. They kept her going with their unending supply of energy and wit, but she was also tired to the point not even sleep nor caffeine couldn't save her. Endless emails, questions, lessons, stacks of papers, nurse's forms, meetings, trainings, and calls were just a typical Monday.

"Just another day at da rock," as her coworker would smile and say, walking down the same hall as he had as a teacher when she was a student. Faded remnants of autographs, warm wishes, and drawings left behind on her bulletin board above a sword of lingering Expo markers reminded her why she continued. Her kids who started the tradition graduated from high school a few weeks ago. How was that possible when they were just in Kori's classroom, learning alongside her? Now, their lives had raced just as she'd warned hers did. Biting down on another cuticle, she desperately rummaged through her things for any distraction from the gnawing ache in her chest.

Kori took her purple polaroid camera out of her tote bag, thinking back to when she and her sister, Katie, had their pictures taken with these instant cameras when they were young. Her favorite was when their cousin captured them jumping on their grandma's bed during the holidays. While the pictures lacked sharpness and detail, they were authentic and sentimental. Her fiancé surprised her with this camera to capture summer memories through the familiar lens. That and writing would keep her busy enough not to dwell too long on the pain of missing the past.

Now for the perfect subject. She looked around the classroom through her viewfinder until she spotted it. Ah, yes. The infamous "G-Unit" desk. The legendary piece of furniture had been in the establishment long before she'd become a middle schooler, and it found its way back to her as a teacher. With the phrase permanently engraved in the top left corner and years of gum-balls underneath—if one dared to behold—it was a true masterpiece and key contribution to the collection of aged classroom materials, such as the 1970's rusted metal cabinets and bookcases. Kori moved closer to the desk, angled the camera to where it leveled with the top, and slanted enough to stretch the phrase across the center of the shot. Once she steadied the camera, Kori pressed down on the shutter button. After a click followed by a brief flash, the camera released the finished product. Kori gently pulled the picture out from underneath the film shield and carefully placed the cloudy result on her desk to finish developing.

She opened her journal but found only starkness. The camera beside it seemed to watch her, patient and expectant. She should've known what to write, but as any writer knows, sometimes the page remains blank no matter how full their heart is. The camera seemed to stare back at her. Kori picked it up, turned the power button on, stretched her arms out, tilted her head slightly to the left as she always had out of habit, and snapped the picture. She'd nearly seen stars after forgetting to turn the flash off but still managed to pull the picture out from underneath the film shield and set it beside the other. Like everything else that day, she'd have to wait like her childhood self, eager for summer's first taste.

"Did you take your mobile lab down to the computer room?" Quinn asked from her doorway, bringing her back to the present. His bright hazel eyes locked in on her vacant stare. As always, he knew. "You're stuck with your writing, aren't you?"

Kori rubbed her temples, then pulled her highlighted hair up into a classic messy bun and rested her head on the desk. "Ugh. Is it that obvious? I—"

"Nope! C'mon!" He interrupted, marching across the classroom. Quinn pulled her to her feet and took the cart with his other hand. "We're going to clear our minds and send tech on wheels down the hall before the custodians start waxing the rooms. We can walk and talk."

The guy knew what she needed. They'd been the best of friends since college and were lucky enough to work in the same school years later. Together, the two lived the American dream until 3:40 P.M. then briefly escaped to each other's fictional universes, evaluating and critiquing character development and conflict. Both struggled to manifest the slightest ounce of creativity during the demanding days that followed spring break until the final signature on the sign-out sheet in the office.

Quinn pushed the cart down the half-lit hall, past a series of flipped desks. "So, something's got ya down. Care to talk about it, or would you prefer a temporary distraction before revisiting the subject?"

Kori rolled her eyes and laughed, "Surprise me?"

"Okay, since we're now passing the nurse's office, we're ripping off that Band-Aid. Pour the tea. What's going on?"

"What does the nurse's office have to do wi—"

"Eh. No-no, dear. No deflections," Quinn interrupted, effortlessly weaving the lab cart through the obstacle course of discarded chairs, bookcases, and stacks of empty boxes. "Let the emotional support bestie do his thing. We're going to talk this out, and if I need to whack the audacity out of anyone, that can also be arranged."

Kori opened the door to the computer room for Quinn. The overwhelming "tropical" scent of industrial disinfecting spray stung both her nostrils and eyes.

"It's nothing big or anything. I mean... I miss the kids, but I'm also ready for summer as always," she said, covering her nose and mouth with her jacket sleeve. "But like this time of year, I kinda miss the old days... you know... being kids, family vacations, birthday parties, going to the park. Now, it's all catching up on cleaning and starting random house projects. I swear... sometimes ... it feels like we just woke up one day and were suddenly adults."

Quinn slowly nodded, propping his elbow on top of the cart and rubbing his chin. "A little heavy on the rambling, but yeah... life moves pretty fast. Your problem is you're like me and don't take any YOU time. Why not use that for your writing? Go down 'memory lane' for inspiration while you find your story."

He had a point. Writing wasn't the same as living an event, even with a vivid imagination, but at least it would be better than nothing. "So, what about you? How are you doing?"

Quinn glanced at his smart watch. "Well, I have my final evaluation in five minutes. After that, I'll have my last signature, and then I'm making a spice-free dinner at Gram's because God forbid we have flavor. Ugh I—" The alarm on Quinn's smart watch aggressively buzzed. "Well, crap!" He repeatedly tapped the screen to stop the alarm. "I apparently have my meeting now. I'll call you later! Love you, byeee!" Quinn hurried out of the room and to the office.

"Love you, too. Byeee!" Kori laughed and headed down the hall in the opposite direction, back to her classroom. Even more desks and chairs were stacked along the lockers. Thankfully, hers remained in place for now. The polaroids sitting beside her journal turned out slightly blurred but still visible. Kori flipped the photo in her hand. The "G-Unit" mark was still there, but now something else new shimmered beneath it. A butterfly? She leaned in, her heart skipping. That wasn't there before.

Then, the room shifted. The air surrounding her buzzed faintly, like the static before a storm. The butterfly glowed like a bolt of lightning without a source for its illumination. A prism of pastel hues emitted from the photo with sharpening pixels, until a soft white glow reached out toward her, soft and warm like an embrace. Darkness fell upon her.

When Kori awoke, everything changed. The desk beneath her was smaller, yet familiar. The classroom walls returned to the original butter yellow filled with old grammar and inspirational posters. *Have a great summer!* was neatly written in fresh blue chalk on the board. The date in the corner was *June 6, 2005*. Subtle hints of the school's famous square pizzas and burnt popcorn wafted through. She was there. Twenty years ago. In her very classroom. Kori's composition notebook sat in the middle of her desk. She flipped through the pages to the last entry:

June 5, 2005

I used to be afraid of the future. I don't know what I want to be, but maybe that's part of how life goes. Next year is my last year at KPMS, and it's crazy how fast time flew. I've been here since kindergarten. The time in high school is even less. After only four years, we'll leave again.

We were told to put a picture with this entry. One that meant a lot to us. I decided to share this photo of my Nanny and me. She wanted to be a writer, just like me, but didn't get the chance. Nanny was kind and loving, and I don't ever remember fighting with her. She'd always say, "Hi sugar!" when she saw my sister and me and gave us the best vanilla with chocolate fudge swirl ice-cream and Sprite. I felt like my happiest days were gone once she died. I wasn't even out of primary school yet. I miss those summers.

It's not the same, but I try to make the most of it because I know that's what she'd want. Now Granddad's cancer is getting worse.

I don't know how much time we have left, but we'll make it count. That's all we can do. It always hits hardest on the last day, but I'll give tomorrow a chance.

Kori hadn't realized just how much she'd felt the same in the past as she had in the present.

The simplest days would always be when she was little, running barefoot in the backyard in sunflower dresses, chasing butterflies and hoping to hold one. They were the most innocent and sentimental, but life continued and things changed. All seasons had their moment in the sun, the sorrow with joy. Her teacher, Mrs. Aldridge, left a note in red pen at the bottom of the page:

Kori, every day is a new day. Each summer has an opportunity for adventure if you take it. Have a great summer! 100%

Wise words from a kind teacher whom she'd adored and now strived to continue her legacy in the same room. Once again, the magic of the room helped inspire her. Kori gazed at the taped picture of her and her nanny. Nanny rocked an infant Kori in her living room's recliner, smiling down at her. A paper and pen sat on the armrest. Something was written on it with some scribbled out phrases. She tried to read it but couldn't make out the cursive in the angle the picture was taken.

Kori carefully removed the tape that held the picture to the notebook page and tried to focus on the writing in hopes to at least make out a phrase. The same glowing prism of pastel shades emitted from the picture, and the pixels sharpened until a shimmering white light stretched out toward her. Kori briefly closed her eyes, then opened them to her childhood living room. Only, this time, the pastel shades remained like a dreamy 35 mm film. Her favorite Home Sweet Home candle with the sweetest spices filled the room. She now stood beside the recliner, where her nanny rocked an infant Kori until she yawned and snuggled against her in a soothing sleep. Her nanny gently smiled down at her and used her free hand to continue writing on the paper on the armrest.

Remember just one thing, dear child.

God is always near.

Love,

Nanny

She set the pen on top of the paper, and continued rocking. A tear ran down Kori's cheek as she smiled at them. She wiped her eyes and sighed as a cooling sensation swept over the gnawing ache in her chest until only peace remained. For someone who never saw the true value in their words or actions, her Nanny always shared sincere encouragement when it was most missed and needed. The evening sunlight streamed through a nearby window and illuminated a vivid sapphire blue butterfly brooch around her neck. It had the same long wings as the one in her photograph.

The selfie polaroid fell to her feet. On its surface, the butterfly reappeared as a sketch on the whiteboard behind her. Kori knelt, picked it up, and held it close. This time, she was ready. A shimmering prism of vibrant colors emitted from the picture, casting long, soft shadows across the room until everything blurred.

Then, only silence. Stillness.

Kori slowly opened her eyes. Her cheek rested on her desk beside her purple polaroid camera, pictures, and journal. She was back, or had she even left? Either way, things would be well. She knew that now. Two timelines lived within, and that was okay. Her childhood with family was brief, and adulthood seemed fleeting. A desperate desire to cling to sentimental remnants of her home dug its talons into her heart, fearing how much longer she had. Teaching her students revived the joy of the simpler times but also forewarned the transient nature of each season.

"Just wanted to check in before I head out," Quinn said, walking over to Kori's desk, "How are you?"

Kori took a deep breath and grinned, "Better."

"Good. Let's see that journal."

Kori opened her journal to the first page. A bright blue butterfly with long, delicate wings fluttered in through the open window and landed on the top right corner.

She beamed. All those years, she'd chased butterflies only to find they'd never left her nor ever would.

"Looks like I have a story to write."

Not just about the past—but also the present, and everything in between.

Life wasn't simpler back then, just different. And the present? That was enough.

24

SWARM

BY A. L. PAOLUCCI

When silence rings
And the world stills
Alone with my thoughts
The flies swarm

They mock the pen, the brush, my hands
Belittling my imagination
Buzzing in my ears, rattling my brain
The flies swarm

Blurs of grays spiral around
Vibrations of degrading chants
Bad words, bad pictures, bad creations of hands
No good, never good, hopeless, give up
They swarm

Yet a sliver of color arrives
Carried by delicate wings
Fluttering with grace and grit
A butterfly slips through the swarm

Her whispers are faint, yet they are there
Make words, make pictures, make with hands
No matter good or bad, shape and mold
Overcome the swarm

New hope, deep breath, release
I pick up the pen, the brush
Ready my hands
I create

25

WINGS OF INK

BY ADELE LILES

My mother spoke of butterflies like they were promises,
a delicate map of all the places she dreamed of going
but never could—
each wing a whisper of freedom
she swore she'd wear on her skin someday.

She'd trace the curve of her hip,
saying, "Right here, where no one can see,
except for me, when I need a reminder."
But the years passed,
and her hip stayed bare.

When she died,
the air felt too still,
like the world had lost the flutter of her dreams.
Her voice lingered in the empty corners,
the ghost of her *someday* left unfinished.

So I sat in a chair beneath buzzing needles,
the hum like the murmur of wings,

and let the artist press my mom's memory into my flesh,
transforming my grief into a tether
fluttering against my heartbeat.

The ink etched her longing into my skin,
a butterfly she never wore,
its wings spreading across my hip
as if to say,
"Now, you can carry me wherever you go."

And every time I look in the mirror,
I see her dreams in flight—
a promise fulfilled in shades of purple.
And I swear, for a moment,
I feel the flutter of her hand on mine.

26

I WAS NEVER REALLY HERE

BY AMANDA DODGE

Dried shards of blue wings suspended in a gossamer web fluttered one last time against the cracked window. The nozzle of the vacuum cleaner slurped away the accumulated debris that had come with her mother's declining health. With her mother's insistence that she was fine and didn't need help.

Don't trouble yourself. I know you're busy.

Had she been?

Matilda didn't know. Every minute tumbled away from her with a promise that tomorrow would be better. She would become all the things she always wanted to be and take care of everything she'd put off. But in forty-six years of living, she hadn't managed to do a single thing she'd meant to.

An ache throbbed in her arm as she lifted the ancient Hoover to reach every nook and cranny of her mother's drafty old cottage. The same seaside home Matilda had fumbled through her adolescence. Her childhood had been happy in ways that meant there was nothing wrong, no external trauma that had whittled away at her identity.

Nothing to explain why she was the way she was. She had been loved and cared for. But she had never been right, never been happy.

Matilda didn't like returning to the place she had shed. The unexplainable loneliness that still lingered in the wood, calling to her. She welcomed the whine of the vacuum. It filled the space, silenced her thoughts and dampened her grief, a grief she should have felt three months ago when they pulled her mother's body from the sea.

The memories surfaced, unwelcomed, shuffled, and out of order, her mother three years ago, sitting at the kitchen table, coffee growing cold between her hands. "I feel like I'm disappearing, Matti. Like I was never really here to begin with."

Matilda had glanced up from her phone, muttered something about getting older, and missed the meaning entirely. Now she understood her mother had been trying to tell her about the diagnosis, about the fog already beginning to creep in.

A flash of blue caught her eye. A butterfly, impossible in October, fluttered past the window, then disappeared.

Then came the call a few months back in one of her mother's final lucid moments. "You box everything up so neat and tidy in that head of yours."

Matilda had promised to visit soon and ended the conversation, telling herself she'd call back tomorrow. Tomorrow became next week. Next week became her biggest regret, the notification from the police.

Matilda's second biggest regret to date was her inability to really explain how she felt. To her mother. To anyone. Let alone in a situation where her mother's death crept about the house, watching her from around the corners, waiting to see how she would react.

How could she explain the images that gave shape to the world inside her? She certainly felt things. But when it came to composing her features, to pouring out all the things that swirled inside her, her tongue twisted into knots, a useless pink hunk.

It paralyzed her some days. Other days she could pull the puppet strings of her being mirroring smiles and eye contact, convincing others that she too was a human, until she felt as empty and hollowed out as a marionette.

She jabbed the foot pedal of the vacuum, the loneliness rushing in to fill the silence. She dabbed at the sweat on her forehead as it prickled and itched. Without warning, tears bubbled up, and she hugged herself, the weight of it all threatening to collapse her.

She sucked in air as noisily and graciously as the vacuum, making the box in her mind.

Breathe in for four. Hold for four. Out for four. Hold for four.

Once the breaths tidied her emotions away, she coiled up the vacuum cord, snaking it neatly around the little arms meant to hold it, and tossed away the bag fat with cobwebs and dust.

Trash bags weighed down her hands as she swung them into the cargo area of her Subaru. The windows watched her mournfully, as if they feared she would leave and never return. Its emptiness wrapped around her.

What was she going to do now? She couldn't live in this house. Couldn't sell it. There were too many markings in the walls that told the story of her life, but at the same time, she didn't want to read them—didn't want someone else to read them, either.

Her phone rang. The generic do-da-do ringer made her jump. Her heart tumbled out of her chest and flopped around the sandy drive like a fish. She blinked, and the beating hunk of flesh was safely returned to her imagination.

The 207-area code meant it was local, so she answered.

"Matti?" Ross's voice was older now, frayed at the edges like a sweater she couldn't bring herself to get rid of because it felt so right against her skin. No one called her Matti in New York.

"Ross?" his name toppled down the staircase of her mouth.

"Good to know you haven't forgotten my name," he laughed, and her heart stuttered. "I heard you were in town. I just wanted to check in... see if you needed anything. It's what your mom would have wanted."

Ross was on the phone with her, and her mother was dead. But nothing about this felt real; her mother wasn't dead, she was inside.

A gull cried somewhere behind her as the sea scraped along the shore, grounding her for a second. "I'm fine... just getting things in order." He didn't need to know the dirty details. Her not sleeping, her hurt, the things she'd been seeing. It could all stay balled up inside her.

"Will you sell the place? I could lend a hand getting it ready. Your mom was like a mother to me when we were kids. It's the least I could do."

Ross had practically lived with them. Both their dads had been fishermen, out to sea during the day and in the bars at night. His mom was a bartender who always smelled of cherries and cigarettes. Even now, Matilda could picture her clearly, crop tops or leather, big hair that never smelled of hairspray. Matilda had liked the way she chewed gum. There was something about the way her jaw rolled the edible plastic around, daring someone to pick a fight with her. The complete opposite of her house dress wearing, apron clad mother. Always cleaning, always worrying, and throwing her arms around Matilda, suffocating her with kisses.

“It’s fine, really,” she said. The space between her words silently overflowed with *please come* and *I don’t know what I’m doing*.

“You sure? I know it’s been a minute since we’ve seen each other, but your mom and I kept in touch. We were close.”

We were close. His words tugged at her chest, the peeling off of a scab she thought was ready only to reveal a still raw wound. Of course, they were close. Everyone was close, everyone knew how to be, except for her.

“Okay. Come for dinner then.” She cupped her forehead, feeling the two decades that had passed since she’d last seen him in the wrinkles on her brow. “Six-thirty.”

“Do you still like Rolling Rock?”

She could hear his crescent moon smile.

“Oh god.” She pulled her sweater up to cover her face, even though he couldn’t see her.

A montage of moonlit green bottles on the beach flickered in her mind. Bonfires that were tall enough to set the stars ablaze. A tanned boy and a freckled girl, limbs tangling in the sand, uncertain but ready to find out.

“I’ll bring some, just in case. See ya soon.” He hung up before she could reply, and butterflies battled in her belly.

Ross had been her first friend, first love, first of everything, including heartbreak. He had loved this place, loved the sea too much to follow her to concrete jungles and possibilities that meant he didn’t have to come home smelling of fish and diesel.

But she had left because she needed something and

never looked back, still her happiness had turned to salt. And his? Was he happy?

The cottage door creaked open to a flash of silver hair, stormy sea eyes, and a white nightgown before the door slammed. Matilda slipped the phone into the back pocket of her jeans.

"Mom?" She raced inside, but her mother was nowhere. Matilda squeezed her eyes tight, releasing the tension. "Mom, what are you doing?"

Wet footprints trailed in chaotic paths through the house. Had she gotten water and spilled it? Matilda grabbed a towel from the kitchen and dried the tracks as she passed through the small living room. The vacant wicker furniture watched as she worked down the hall to her mother's bedroom. Gray light spilled into the darkened hall through a crack in the door. Her heartbeat filled the silence as she went in. Her mother lay in bed, but something was different since she last checked on her.

A thin gauzy blanket was wrapped around her, but that wasn't the oddest thing, tucked into the folds of the blanket were photos and trinkets.

Matilda crept into the room, not wishing to disturb her mother. Had she really just bolted through the house? She couldn't reconcile the frail bones moving with such speed.

How had she not slipped?

She edged closer, shaky fingers reaching for the items on display. Curled photos of her mother and father somewhere on a windswept beach, draped in black and white, their contagious smiles curving up her own lips. One of Matilda as a baby, wrapped in crochet from head to toe, nestled in her grandfather's arms. She barely remembered the man. He died when she was little. Now he was a ghost of a memory that smelled of pipe tobacco and coffee. There were other less familiar things, tarnished collector spoons, a change purse, a tube of lipstick that looked like it was from the sixties, and an ornament she had made, her little handprint preserved in the cracked white dough *Xmas '81* etched in the back.

Why had she gone through the trouble to get these things? Did she think she could take them with her like the Egyptians?

Her mother's eyes were open, watery gray seas staring at her—through her.

"Ahhh." Matilda clutched her chest to keep her heart from escaping. "Mom, are you okay? Why did you bring all this stuff in here?"

"I was never really here," she said, her voice ragged and croaky.

"What? What's with the water? If you need something, just ring the bell. I'll get it for you."

"Just be."

"Just be what?" There was no way of knowing whether her mom was lucid or not. And every word fell somewhere in the desperate cracks of hope for one last moment and grief for what had already passed.

"Just be h..." Her words dissolved in a sigh, eyes closed again, lips dry and cracked. Matilda cradled her face and exhaled against her palms. She straightened and went to collect the items to place on her bedside table when her mother grabbed her wrist. Her bony hand was so cold, so frail and thin, the black veins visible through her crepe paper skin. But her eyes were still closed. Matilda dropped the photo and stepped back, her hand falling limply to her mother's side.

"Fine, you keep it. I'll check on you again in a little while. Ross is coming for dinner. I'm sure that makes you happy. He was always a favorite of yours." Her words were met with silence. "Okay, I'll be back. I love you."

Matilda closed the door behind her, then sighed and pressed her back against it. Grief had been a puzzle she never figured out. When her father died ten years ago, it had been swift, reality shattering, and unexpected. Her grief had slipped through the broken pieces, but this was long. And Matilda hadn't been able to face it. Couldn't face her mother not knowing her own daughter and not even knowing herself.

It was half-past three and Ross would be there before she knew it. She regretted accepting his offer. What would he think of her after all this time? She didn't even know if he was married. Her mother had never spoken of him, and Matilda had never asked. Hadn't wanted to know. She lived her nine-to-five life as an accountant in a sensibly modern and tiny apartment in New York City. Her work was fully remote, and though she could live anywhere, she couldn't bring herself to go. But like most things in her life, none of that mattered now.

She showered, massaging the shampoo into her scalp, rinsing thoroughly to ensure no dust or debris lingered. The water lulled. The sound of it raining down her body and onto the tile relaxed her, but heavy footsteps thwacking down the hall outside the bathroom jolted her in a panic. Soapy and afraid, she wrapped a towel around herself and crept into the hall. No one was there. She peered around the corner to her mother's room, and the door was open. Relief eased the rattling in her chest.

"Mom, you shouldn't be out of bed," she called, but there would be no answer. Matilda gave the rest of the house a cursory search before darting to her mother's bedroom, her damp feet leaving prints behind her.

Her mother lay in bed. But as before, she'd swaddled another gauzy blanket around herself, hiding her face. In the folds of the new shroud were more tidbits from around the house. A whisk, a pair of baby shoes Matilda had never seen, a pen, a small music box, and reading glasses. The music box was a delicate driftwood box; a butterfly etched on the lid. Matilda turned it over and cranked the key three times, then opened the lid. A tinny and distorted Brahms' Lullaby poured out, a series of notes like the fluttering of so many wings around her, growing closer and closer until the door behind her slammed shut and she snapped the lid of the music box closed.

"Must have been the draft," she said, suddenly frozen. Matilda returned the box to her mother, who had not stirred. "I'm going to finish my shower. No more sneaking about. I don't want you to get hurt, okay?"

Bracing herself with a steady breath, she returned to the bathroom to finish her shower. Once cleaned up and hair dried, she stared at her freckled face. Were freckles still cute when you were nearly fifty? She could have googled it, but doubted she would like the answers.

Matilda pulled her mass of copper hair back into a clip. What would Ross look like after all these years? The movie reel in her mind flickered through time, fast forwarding the twenty-something frozen in her mind to a man, a sea dog beard like his father, his sandy blonde hair softened to a dishwater blond that masked the gray. He was handsome, he had always been handsome. And yet, he'd liked her. Something she'd never understood and could never give voice to, too afraid she'd break the spell.

In the kitchen, she put water on to boil for pasta as she quickly doctored up a jar of sauce. The heat from the stove stole the nip from the air, and she relished, finally feeling warm as the aroma of basil and garlic wrapped around her.

Gravel crunched outside at exactly six-thirty. Matilda had just checked on her mother, still tucked away beneath her blankets, before taking a final glance at her reflection in the mirror. She opened the door. A smile crested his lips as their eyes locked. He strode toward her, a thumb hooked in his jeans pocket, the other hand holding a six-pack of Rolling Rock that made her laugh despite herself. No wedding ring, but that meant little these days. He looked almost exactly as she imagined. His skin still held a tan, perfectly sea weathered and creased in a rugged way. His curls, dishwater blond, spilled out from under his navy beanie that matched his cable-knit sweater. But there was no scrappy sea dog beard as she'd guessed, just a dusting of snowy scruff along his sharp jaw. She wanted to reach out and touch it.

"Well, don't just gawk at me, get over here," he said, holding his arms open and pulling her into his solid chest. And for reasons she couldn't pinpoint, a sob wracked her body. But he didn't recoil. He cupped the back of her neck, his scratchy cheek pressed to hers as he let her cry. When she collected the pieces of her dignity from the doorway, she motioned for him to come inside, dabbing her eyes with the back of her hand.

"I'm sorry," she said, but he waved her off.

"Don't. That's what I'm here for."

Gratitude welled in her chest, and she wanted to tell him, wanted to confess all the things trapped inside her, but nothing came. Over dinner, they traded stories the way kids at summer camp did. Trying to fit a lifetime of friendship in as little time as possible. It was as if they'd never been apart and like they'd never met all at once. The old ties cocooned them, making them into something old but new.

They were in the middle of washing dishes, the lines of their bodies drawing closer together as she washed and he dried.

"So why'd you never marry?" she asked, but regretted it the moment the words left her lips.

"Who says I didn't?"

"Ah, so you're married?"

"Divorced and single," he said with a little smirk and an arched brow. "We were only married for a few years. She moved south, and I stayed."

"Is that how all your relationships end?"

He laughed, a charming grin showing off his pearly whites. "Just about. How about you?"

How much should she share? She had taken men and women as lovers, but nothing else. No one had made her feel the way he had. Ross had always been her anchor. With him, she didn't get lost in her imagination, in her stuck feelings. But before she could form an answer, the sound of fabric ripping and glass shattering filled the air. She dropped the pan she'd been washing into the sink, sending soapy water flying as she ran to her mother's bedroom.

Ross called after her, "Matti, what's the matter?"

"Didn't you hear that sound? I have to see if she's all right."

She flicked on the lights, the dim yellow glow puddling in the hall. Matilda pushed open the door to the bedroom and stepped inside. A silvery moon glinted off the objects collected in her mother's bed. Sea breeze flooded in through a broken window, the curtain whipping and shredding on the shards of glass.

Her mother was gone. The gauzy layers she'd been

shrouded in flayed open, the trinkets that had made up her mother's life left behind. In her place, an azure butterfly flapped its wings.

Gooseflesh rippled over Matilda's skin as she stared through the broken window. The door slamming came back to her, the constant chill in the house. The window had been shattered since she arrived, and her mother had been dead.

Had she cared for a ghost?

Ross stepped into the room. "What sound? Check on who?"

As if activated by his words, the butterfly fluttered off the bed and out the broken window.

"Jeez, no wonder the house is freezing. And look at that water damage on the floor. The window must've been broken for some time."

"She was never really here," Matilda said. The shock of it all shifted something inside her, freeing her.

Ross rested a warm hand on her shoulder. "I know what you mean. It's scary how quickly it feels like they never existed. She's been gone, what, three months now?"

Her eyes burned, unwilling to cry more than she had that week. She'd finally come to clean up the cottage after her mother had wandered out into the sea and drowned. But she hadn't been dead. She had been there waiting in bed, waiting for her daughter to do the right thing and care for her mother.

The reality in her mind and the one outside fought for purchase. Had she been caring for a ghost? Or had her grief created what she needed, a chance to say goodbye, to be the daughter she'd failed to be in life? She knew with certainty that something had been mistaken, but perhaps the love, the final moments of care, had been real in the way that mattered most.

"Why don't you go relax and I'll tidy this up. Tomorrow, I'll drive over to Ellsworth and get the stuff to fix it. No worries."

If only she could tell him what had really happened.

Matilda finished washing and drying the dishes to the sound of straw bristles scraping glass into the dustpan as Ross worked.

The tears tried to come again as Ross appeared. He dumped the glass in the bin and pulled her in for another hug. "Grief is a strange thing. They say it's a cycle, but it's more like a boomerang."

She burrowed into him, never wanting to emerge again.

"Hey, how about we build a fire on the beach and have a couple of beers for old time's sake? Yeah?"

Ross had a way of making things so easy. Bundled up in an Afghan as the waves crashed in the distance, he built a fire, though not as big as the ones they'd built as kids.

The beers popped and hissed as he twisted off the tops. He handed her one, hovering his near her. "To the ones who are no longer with us."

She clinked her bottle against his and took a long swig. The beer tasted watery and not as good as she remembered.

Something unsaid settled between them, mingling with the crackling of the pine logs and the distant yipping of coyotes.

"I would have gone with you," he said so suddenly, she almost second guessed whether he'd spoken at all. "I was scared, scared of failing. Here, I couldn't fail. I knew I could fish and get by. But you were so brave, I didn't have time to catch up, and by the time I did, you were gone." For a moment he was that boy who'd stolen her heart, but that boy dissolved in the flickering of the firelight.

"But I was never happy in the city."

Three little lines knit between his brow from her words. It felt good to say what she meant.

"How come you stayed away?" There was no heat or judgment in his words, just genuine curiosity.

She picked at the beer label with her thumbnail. "I didn't know what else to do. Every day fell into the next. And I thought, *tomorrow I will make things different*. But it never happened."

He shifted his weight. "There's all this pressure to make it, leave your mark on the world, but really all you should want is to be happy. Isn't it enough to just be present. Just be happy in the here and now and not worry about the next thing."

"Easier said than done."

She thought of her mother, of the miscellaneous items that made up her life. If she were dying, what would she want to take with her? She didn't know, but she was willing to find out.

"What will you do now?" he asked, raising the beer to his lips, the moonlight setting the bottle aglow just the way she remembered. She set her bottle in the sand and inhaled a deep cool breath of salty sea air and wood smoke.

The familiar urge to deflect wriggled inside her. *Say something safe and vague*. The old Matilda would have shrugged and changed the subject. Instead, she took a breath and let herself be uncertain out loud.

"I don't know," she said, surprised by how good it felt to admit it. "But I want to figure it out. Here. Present. Instead of always thinking, tomorrow will be different."

"And what does that mean right now?"

An uncertain smile turned up the corners of her lips. "Well," she said, leaning in, inviting him to meet her halfway, "first I'd like it to entail a kiss."

He cupped her cheek, his calloused thumb tracing her jaw, sending shivers through her as he guided her lips to his. The firelight danced across their faces, and for the first time in as long as she could remember, the world inside her was quiet.

She rested her head on his chest, watching the flames dance with the wind.

"Ross?" she asked, breaking the contented silence. "Do you believe in ghosts?"

27

HOMECOMING

BY LIANNE ROBINSON

The first Sunday in May has always been special to me. It's the day we celebrate Homecoming at our little church. Even now, as I carry several bundles of silk flowers up the hill to the cemetery, I can almost hear the echoes of laughter and the notes of soul-stirring hymns from years ago. I've never missed a Homecoming service at Pine Thicket Baptist Church in all my 84 years.

Folks with starched collars, polished shoes, and fine Sunday dresses will fill the pews tomorrow, but for today, the white clapboard church sits quiet and empty. I glance at the fellowship hall's darkened windows, but my mind goes back to days long gone. I picture them flung open to let the late spring breeze roll through the gauzy curtains while women in floral aprons lined the tables with platters of crispy fried chicken, savory casseroles, and decadent desserts—enough to feed two armies.

I step carefully between the graves, the ground soft from last night's rain. The memories follow me—Uncle Guston slipping me a stick of gum while he folded the wrapper into a fancy silver goblet, Mama whispering warnings about not eating too many sweets, Uncle Red's silly jokes, and the children respectfully tiptoeing through the grassy cemetery as the grown-ups sang "When The Roll Is Called Up Yonder." I still feel that same sense of quiet reverence from long ago as I survey the many headstones laid out under the shady trees. Time did what it always does and stole away everything it touched.

I let out a weary sigh. With everyone in a hurry these days, the church feast isn't what it used to be, and most of the dear souls I remember fellowshipping with are now resting in this sacred ground beneath my feet.

My breath catches and I pause at the edge of the infant burial grounds, where the sunlight twinkles through the pines. The weight of the flowers makes my arms cramp, but my heart aches far more for who waits ahead.

Ava Grace.

I wipe my eyes on my sleeve before I trudge forward. For 55 years, I've cleared away old flowers for Homecoming on Ava Grace's tiny grave. SIDS was a cruel payback for the struggle of a difficult pregnancy. I carried my precious daughter for nine months, but the Lord only let me cradle her in my arms for six weeks. I'll hold her in my heart forever.

I sniffle and breathe in the scent of fresh-cut grass mingled with carnations. The heady fragrance takes me back to Homecomings past, when everyone decorated with live flowers. I miss those days.

I place Ava Grace's new flowers on her headstone and whisper a prayer. My heart beats too hard, filling my ears with a loud cadence of sorrow. Some days it seems like I just lost my girl. Today is one of those times.

In the quiet that follows, my thoughts drift to her father, Michael. He couldn't bear the heartbreak and left me two years after she passed away. I never wanted to remarry or have another child. I thought I couldn't endure the pain of losing anyone else.

But loss has been my only constant companion. I've outlived most of my family, so the grave caretaking responsibilities now fall on me. Today is the day for cleaning the family plots and placing the new flower arrangements. Leaving the rest of the new flowers in a heap on a bench, I walk to the dumpster in the red clay bluffs at the back of the church property to dispose of Ava Grace's faded pink silk flowers. Broken statues, trinkets, and discarded arrangements litter the area. Tattered flowers, most of which are little more than stems, blow in the wind.

"What a mess!" I mumble and shake my head at the church's reluctance to hire a groundskeeper, scowling at the trash. "This is what being cheap gets you."

I grunt as I bend over, gathering all the refuse and tossing it into the overflowing dumpster until something catches my eye. A beautiful blue and purple butterfly flits from one nectarless silk flower to another.

Out of breath from my efforts, I huff, "Oh, come now! You'll starve to death before you find anything to eat here."

The butterfly lands on a pink rose printed on the shoulder of my blouse. "You won't fare any better there, my love. Let me help you."

Hobbling as quickly as my arthritic knees allow, I head to the new section of the cemetery. Since the old section filled up, the deacons recently opened this additional part of the grounds. The grass hardly grows there yet, but the lovely pink and white azaleas along the property line are already in bloom.

I'm surprised the delicate creature remains content to rest on my shirt. She's beginning to look tired and wilted—

just like me. I hope she lives long enough for me to get her to the shrubbery. "Hold on. We're almost there. It's only a few more steps."

Gasping for breath, I reach the top of the small hill and stop when I spot a hearse and the familiar maroon tent of the local funeral home. "Oh dear. I'm interrupting a funeral."

I'm unwilling to create a scene to take the butterfly to the flowers, so I linger in the periphery of the pine tree line. *Whose funeral is this?* I always assist the hospitality committee in serving casseroles and cobblers to the bereaved, but nobody contacted me about this one. *Someone really dropped the ball—probably Sister Gertie.*

I crane my neck to see who the mourners are. I'm puzzled by the familiar faces I recognize. Uncle Red's grandchildren and great-grandchildren occupy two rows of chairs, while Uncle Guston's grandchildren and great-grandchildren fill a row on the opposite side. *I didn't realize they were in town. Why didn't they reach out to me?*

I raise my hand to greet my cousin Alice when I notice her looking my way. But she lowers her head and stares at her lap without acknowledging me. *How rude! Maybe she needs new glasses.*

My waving disturbs the butterfly, causing it to leave my shoulder. Fluttering through the breeze toward the funeral gathering, it lands on an exquisite arrangement of white roses atop the shiny silver casket. The graceful creature drinks deeply before making a return flight to my blouse. "Welcome back, friend. Are you feeling better now?"

It slowly flaps and unfurls its wings to the rhythm of my pastor's prayer.

I strain my ears to hear the name of the deceased, but I still can't identify who they are eulogizing. *I suppose my hearing isn't what it used to be.* I resolve to steal a few steps closer, but not close enough to disturb anyone... *I need to know who this is!* But my feet feel anchored, and I can't move.

Before my frustration boils over, a nearby voice sweetly calls, "Hello." I turn to see who's there as a tiny, warm hand brushes against my fingers. A little girl, appearing to be around 7 or 8 years old, grasps my left hand with both of hers. She wears a satiny white gown adorned with delicate lace and sparkling embroidery. I've never seen anything quite like it. Her light-red hair cascades over her shoulders in tight ringlets. The gorgeous child seems familiar, but I can't quite recall where I know her from. *Maybe she's Sister Gertie's great-granddaughter?*

"Well, hello there. What's your name?"

The little girl smiles and shakes her head. The simple gesture makes my eyes grow damp, but I don't know why.

I shrug and tilt my head to the side. "You won't tell me your name? Okay, then. Who are you here with?"

"You, of course—and that pretty butterfly. Is it your pet?"

I furrow my brow. "Oh, no. She just landed on me. I came up here to find her some flowers to drink from because she was tired and hungry."

"What kind of butterfly is she?"

"You know, I don't know much about butterflies. I only know that they don't live very long. It makes me a little sad."

"Yes," the girl says, smiling. "Sometimes beautiful things can't stay here."

My hand tingles when she squeezes it. *Her green eyes... so much like my own.*

"That's very true." My heartstrings twang at her deep musing—too profound for someone so young. "Little girl, can you tell me whose funeral this is?"

The child purses her rosy lips and pauses for a moment. Finally, she says, "Mama, it's time to go home."

Her words bring a fresh flood of tears to my eyes. A sob escapes my chest as I drop to my knees and gasp at the realization.

Now at eye-level with the angelic child, I stroke the contour of her jaw, every line of her face a perfect echo from my memories. "Hello, Ava Grace. I'm so very happy to see you."

The spirit within me cries out in celebration as my beautiful daughter beams radiantly at me. Together, we watch the butterfly take to the air once more.

She helps me back to my feet and we hold hands again, her soft skin a contrast to my rough, age-mottled hands. She gives me a sideways grin and whispers, "Let's go, Mama."

As they gently lower my casket, we chase the butterfly through the cemetery, skipping and asking pardon as we leap over graves. Sweet, melodic hymns fill the air as we follow the soaring butterfly toward a brilliant beam of sunlight.

I pause, savoring the moment before we take our final step. A peace I haven't felt in decades settles over me, warm and pure. The sorrows that threatened to drown me on the cold, lonely nights now ebb away like a low tide, washing the fierce ache of longing from my soul. I remember now my heart giving out in the night, and my fear in the sudden darkness, but it no longer frightens me. Here, with my daughter smiling at me, my body fills with a joy so full it lifts me heavenward. Being with Ava Grace makes everything right.

This is my favorite Homecoming of all.

28

SETTING FREE

BY HOLLY GOODE

My knuckles whiten with my grip on the steering wheel as I maneuver another treacherous mountain curve. I pretend I do this every day, when in reality, I don't even have a license, and I stole my best friend's beat up car.

Is it really stealing when he's with me?

I loosen my hands enough to reach over to the passenger seat and feel the metal urn holding him. Alex is with me. I will follow through on my promise to spread his ashes so his crappy family can't bring him down any further than they did when he was alive.

The car veers to the left, toward the grass on the edge of the road. I let go of Alex, and regain control, pulling us back to the middle of the pavement where the biggest pothole I've ever seen waits. A scream escapes my lips as I bounce in my seat with the dip. As the noise dies down, my eyes find the flashing red light on the dash. Before I can decipher its meaning, smoke billows through the vents, blinding me.

My lungs revolt with a gasping cough, and I pull to the side of the road, open the door, and jump onto the grass.

Flames bloom from the rusted hood, warming my skin in the autumn breeze.

Of everything that could go wrong, the stupid car decides to not only stop working, but to catch on fire. I've already lost my best friend, now I'm going to lose his ashes.

The mountain breeze carries smoke through the trees surrounding me, and my eyes sting. Do ashes burn away in a fire? Or will they remain, waiting for me in the steel blue urn when this is all said and done?

The sound of oncoming traffic nears. There's never anyone on this road. That's why I chose it. A motorcycle zooms past me, its rider in black leather. The engine roars, and he makes a u-turn, heading back in my direction.

I ignore the stranger as flames surround the car's hood, reaching toward the sky. I can't leave Alex to burn again.

Without taking a breath, I rush back through the open door, reaching aimlessly into the passenger seat. My fingers find the urn, and I tighten my hold as someone pulls on my shoulders, dragging me away from the flames that reach from the dash toward my arms.

A bear of a man stares down at me like I've lost my mind. Maybe I have, but he has no proof of that.

"What are you doing?" he screams, pulling off his helmet. His piercing stare meets mine, and his emerald eyes captivate me. "That car could blow up at any second." He scans my body, searching for injuries. I hide them inside where my grief slumbers night and day.

"My life was in there," I try to explain, clutching the urn to my chest.

The stranger's gaze narrows in on the vessel holding Alex. "I doubt whoever that is would want you to risk your life."

My hands shake, and my breaths quicken, racing my

heartbeat. The stranger is right. Alex would have never wanted me to get hurt for him. Even when he was alive, he was always reminding me to take care of myself.

Tears burn my eyes as they roll down my cheeks. The man's brow furrows. He glances between me and the car. With a shake of his head, he wraps his arm around my shoulders and guides me away from the disaster my life has become.

"Shhhh," he whispers. His deep voice is soothing, nothing like the high-pitched tone Alex had. "It's going to be okay."

I've heard that more times than I can count. It's a lie. Nothing is okay anymore.

I pull away from the stranger and straighten my spine. "I don't need your pity."

His eyebrows raise as he holds his hands out in front of him. "I'm just trying to help."

He removes a phone from his pocket. Before he can dial 911, I reach with lightning-fast speed and jerk it from his hand, then throw it on the ground. The sound of glass shattering fills the air.

The stranger's mouth hangs open. "What are you doing?" His voice rises. He bends down to pick up his phone, stabbing his finger at the broken screen. His glare deepens as the device refuses to cooperate.

I cringe. I shouldn't have done that, but he can't call for help. If he does, cops will arrive, and I'll be arrested for not only stealing a car, but Alex's ashes. It's not my fault his horrible sister believes she deserves him. Alex couldn't stand being around her when he was alive; he wouldn't want to spend eternity on her mantle.

The stranger scowls as he takes a step toward his bike.

"Wait." My voice cracks. "Please." I may not find another way out of here without him.

He turns to face me, running his hand through his hair, cut in a horrible mullet that makes him look forty when he has to be ten years younger. "I was going to help, but you destroyed my phone."

A boom sounds through the forest. I throw my hands over my face, ducking as the car explodes and heat rushes up my exposed arm. Before I can open my eyes, I'm pulled closer to the trees.

A cold chill spreads across my arms as I stare at the mess I was almost inside of. The car's rusted paint is unrecognizable. Not only am I a thief, but now I'm an arsonist. Tomorrow's headline runs through my mind: *Crazy friend steals deceased ashes and car, burning them both to the ground in a fit of rage.*

"What am I going to do?" I whisper.

The man meets my gaze. "What's your name?"

"Amanda." The word floats away on the smokey breeze surrounding us.

"Do you have a phone?"

I shake my head, and his eyes narrow.

"I lost it," I lie. The truth won't help me now. I couldn't bring a phone with me on this mission. Phones are too easy to track.

"I'm James. My house isn't far from here. I'll take you there, and we can find some help."

As if on autopilot, I nod. It isn't smart to go with a stranger, but what choice do I have?

James runs his hand through his hair, and a deep sigh slips between his lips.

"You would look a lot better with a haircut." The words tumble out, and I cover my mouth as my face warms. "I'm sorry. That was rude. I haven't been myself lately. Not since..." My words trail off. I look down at the silver container in my hands.

A slight laugh fills my awkward silence. "I've told my producers that, but they never listen."

Producers? Before I can question him, he turns and walks toward the bike. I trail behind like a lost puppy.

He passes his black helmet to me. "It's going to be too big, but I don't have another."

I push it away. "You should wear it then." I couldn't have saved Alex, but if James wrecks, and I have his helmet, I'll never forgive myself.

The muscles in James' strong jaw flex as he shakes his head. "You're not getting on my bike without a helmet."

I shrug, pulling the sweaty thing over my head. It's way too large and moves up and down, but James seems satisfied as he swings his leg over the bike. He kicks the stand, and the muscles in his thighs bulge against his tight pants. I clamber behind him, placing Alex between his back and my chest.

A sharp pain crosses my chest. I should be mourning Alex, not ogling a man I just met, no matter how attractive he is.

James reaches back, grabbing my arm, and tugging me into his spine. "Hold on."

My fingers tighten around his abs, and I close my eyes as Alex's voice rings in my ears.

Just enjoy life, Amanda. You don't have to be miserable all the time.

Tears burn, falling down my cheeks as the motorcycle coasts along the curved mountain roads. Instead of turning left toward the nearest highway, James keeps right, zooming up the mountainside. I push my head into his back to block my vision as I pray I won't get sick. The twists and turns were bad enough in a car, but on two wheels, I may empty my stomach.

"We're almost there," James says. His hand falls on top of mine. He presses it harder into his abdomen, reminding me to tighten my grip.

We pull through a large iron gate. The metal twists into wings that float in the air. Butterflies, I realize as the bike slows on the brick road.

I shift back, gawking at a mansion that could hold twenty of my apartments. The bike comes to a halt in front of the white double door. James loosens my grip on his shirt and flashes me a wide smile as he jumps off the bike. I remove his helmet and stare at the house.

"You don't know who I am, do you?" James asks.

Should I? Does he recognize me? I'm sure the theft of an urn is all over social media.

James clears his throat. He tilts his head, and a dimple draws my gaze. My mouth drops open.

"James Monroe," we say at the same time.

A small laugh leaves his lips as the air in my lungs escapes at the sight of the legend in front of me.

The James Monroe.

I can hear Alex yelling at me to get it together as if he were beside me instead of in a container on my lap. *Say something witty! Tell him how much we loved his performance in Cars Getaway 2.*

My vision blurs, and I internally groan. Alex loved every one of James Monroe's movies while I sat through them, bored, praying for a gorgeous elf to swoop in and save the princess instead of action and fighting. I blink, trying to clear my mind as pins and needles jet across my skin.

James' eyes narrow. "Are you okay?"

I open my mouth to lie, but the edges of my vision darken. I blink hard, trying to gain control as the world tilts on its axis, and his muscular arms wrap around me.

"I DON'T KNOW WHAT HAPPENED!" a masculine voice says. "She just collapsed."

I peek through the slits of my eyelids, and dim light fills my vision. A soft cushion lies underneath me. I prop up on my elbows, looking around the room.

I have to be dreaming. There's no way I'm inside James Monroe's house.

My throat throbs as I try to clear it. It can't be a dream if I feel pain.

"No one saw me," James says. He's pacing around a large wooden table set for ten. "What did you want me to do? Leave her there to burn to death?" He must be talking to his producer. The stupid one that demands he keep his hideous haircut. "No one ever goes down that road. She would have been stranded for hours."

James freezes, and the muscles in his jaw tighten as he removes the phone from his ear, ending the call. His fingers whiten as they wrap around the plastic.

I cringe. I broke his other phone, and there's no way I can repay him for it.

As if he can feel my eyes on him, he turns to me, and I meet his deep green stare.

"You're up! Are you okay?" He rushes to my side.

Before I can speak, his arms are around my back. I sit up on the leather sofa that fills the living quarters. Instead of a TV, a wall full of bookcases is the centerpiece.

James kneels in front of me, blocking my view of the

titles. His brows nearly meet as he passes me a bottle of water. I take a sip, and the cool liquid clears my burning throat.

"Are you okay, Amanda?" he asks again.

I look toward the phone clutched in his hand. "You have another one?"

"Uhh, yeah." He drops it on the side table as if it were acid. "This one is just for the producers. They like to be able to get in touch with me even when I don't want to hear from them."

I nod, as if this is everyday life.

James moves a step away from me. "Do you want me to call someone?"

I shake my head. There's no one to call. I've never been good at making friends, and my family has had nothing to do with me in years. It was just Alex and me. Now, it's just me.

"Are you sure?"

"I'll be okay," I lie. "I can get an Uber."

I push off the sofa, and the room sways. James shoots forward. His fingers find the small of my back as he guides me to the couch. My stomach turns. I haven't had an actual meal since Alex died, and surviving on chips isn't working anymore.

"What do you need?" James asks. His voice is deep, just like it is in the movies.

I need to get away. I need to find a new place to live since I can't stand staying in the apartment Alex and I shared. It's not like I could afford it on my own anyways.

My gaze darts around the space, searching for the urn holding my friend.

"I put it on the table," James says, somehow knowing what I was thinking. "Why don't I make us some sandwiches, then you can call that Uber?" He turns on his heel and walks toward what I assume is the kitchen.

I would've thought that James Monroe lived in a modern house with stuffy furniture, but the leather couch beneath me is worn and more comfortable than my own bed. The bookshelves call to me, so I force myself to my feet again. This time, I hold my arms out to steady myself if the room spins. It doesn't, allowing me to inch toward the paperbacks.

Books of all genres cover the shelves, not the prestigious classics I expected a millionaire to have. Instead, they're well-read fantasies with cracked spines and dog-eared pages.

"So, what happened with the car?" James' voice booms behind me.

Over my shoulder, I find him holding a mug with a calico cat on it.

"Yours is on the table," he says, nodding toward the dining room.

James pulls out an old wooden chair that has hearts carved into the back.

"Thanks." I settle down and ready my coffee as James returns, carrying two plates piled high with sandwiches.

"I didn't know what you liked, so I made a bit of everything."

The corners of my lips turn up, and I reach out and grab one. I'm so hungry I would eat anything this man offered.

"So?" His brows raise in a way that would make any woman swoon.

"So?"

"The car."

My face falls. The car I stole and accidentally blew up.

"It was my best friend's," I explain, glancing at the urn.

"They're in there?" James motions to the silver container.

I nod. "His name was Alex. We were best friends for as long as I can remember but..." My voice cracks. "He died." A tear rolls down my cheek. Before I can wipe it away, James reaches across the table to remove the evidence of my pain.

"I'm sorry for your loss." Even though he doesn't know me, he sounds sincere.

"The car was his. But his sister took everything when he died. Alex hated her. He couldn't stand to be in the same room with her. He wouldn't have wanted to spend eternity on her mantle watching her judge every friend she pretends she has."

James' eyes widen, and he leans back in his seat as if he needs to distance himself from the criminal he invited into his home.

"She's going to say I stole it," I continue. "But I didn't. I was going to return the car." My words falter, and my gaze darts back to Alex's urn. "I just didn't think it would catch on fire. I don't know what happened. I was driving, and then smoke started coming through the vents. I couldn't see anything."

James takes a sip of his coffee, and his elbow finds the table as he props his chin up on his hand.

I take a breath, knowing I sound crazy. I'm already a thief, but the way his green eyes are looking at me, I have to speak the truth.

"I was trying to give Alex what he asked for," I say. "He wanted his ashes to float away in the mountain breeze. He planned on living on the top of these roads one day, but now he can't."

James passes me a napkin to dry my eyes, then stands and walks to the small table near the door.

He picks up a set of keys. "Come on."

My eyes widen. Is he taking me to the police? I can't blame him if he does. It's what I would do if I were in his shoes.

"If you call them, they'll come get me." I push to my feet. "You don't have to take me to the police station."

James rolls his eyes, and the corners of his lips turn up. "Grab the urn. Let's take that friend of yours on his last adventure. I know the best views around here."

My breath stalls. He isn't going to turn me into the authorities. He's going to help me.

I cradle the urn to my chest as I follow James out the front door. He ignores the bike, walking around the large house toward a garage that could hold ten cars.

"Give me a second," he says, entering the side door.

Before I can catch my breath, the door slides open, and a bright red convertible pulls into the drive.

James' smile matches the ones I used to wear. "You coming?"

I climb into the leather seat before I can second guess myself.

With a full stomach, my nausea remains at bay. The car speeds around a bend, and James stops at a fence blocking a path between giant oak trees that have withstood the test of time. He jumps out and hops over the short gate.

I follow, carrying Alex against my chest. We walk in silence through the tall trees until an opening appears, and the world waits below. My breath stalls at the beauty of the setting sun falling on the mountainside, blanketing the trees in the fiery orange of fall–the same orange that destroyed the car I was in earlier today. A light blue butterfly lands on a dandelion, and a small smile breaks across my lips. In the mess of my life, there is beauty to still be found.

"This is the best view in America," James says. He leans his head back and takes in a breath of fresh air. "Your friend couldn't have picked out a better spot himself."

I smile at the man beside me and open the top of the urn.

He's right. I would have never found this place. It's the exact dream Alex's soul would crave.

James Monroe helped put me to rest.

I hear my friend's voice jet through the trees, and my shoulders relax as I tip the urn over, allowing his ashes to blow away. The butterfly bolts from its perch, and dandelion seeds fill the air as it flies away with my best friend.

He's free. I did exactly as he asked before he left me.

My breath comes lighter, and a soft smile finds its way to my lips.

James' gaze meets mine.

"Thank you," I whisper.

He nods as sirens sound in the distance, growing closer with each second. My shoulders stiffen. I knew I was going to get in trouble for this.

"Let's get out of here before they find us," James says. He stays one step ahead of me, returning us to the world.

I follow behind, putting the top back on the empty urn. I practically jog to keep up with James' long legs, but he helps me across the gate and holds the passenger door open.

Blue lights flash around the bend. James grabs the urn and stashes it beneath the floorboard of the backseat. He pushes me against the car, leaning toward me. My heart races as my breath stalls. I could push him away, but my blood sings at his proximity.

"Do you trust me?" James whispers in my ear.

No, I start to say, but that isn't right. James had more

than one opportunity to harm me. Instead, he's gone out of his way to help me through my toughest day.

I nod, and his lips turn up.

"I'm going to kiss you. If it's too much, push me away," he warns as his lips meet the exposed skin of my neck. My mouth hangs open, and he traces kisses up my jawline. His lips touch mine as the officers invade our space.

The kiss is soft, and his hand brushes the small of my back as he pulls me closer.

James smiles against my mouth and pulls away.

He runs a hand through his hair and turns, flashing his perfectly straight teeth at the three men interrupting.

"Is there a problem, officers?" His voice is velvet.

A short brown-haired man blinks wildly. "Um... Mr. Monroe," he stammers. "We were looking for a criminal we believed was heading this way." They narrow their eyes. "An Amanda Price."

My heart races, but James wraps his arm around my shoulders and gives me a gentle squeeze.

"What did she do?" he asks.

"She stole a car and... an urn," the officer says.

James' laugh echoes through the trees. "You must be confused. Amanda has been with me all day. I picked her up this morning for coffee, and we've been riding these mountain roads thinking of the perfect way to end our evening."

There's no way they believe James, but he's putting on the best act I've ever seen, and I know better than to argue.

The tallest officer narrows his eyes at me. "Did you happen to see an old Corolla on fire during your drive?"

"No, sir," I whisper.

The officer wrinkles his nose as if he can smell the smoke leaching through my clothes, telling the truth we're hiding.

James steps forward, pulling a card from his pocket. "If you need anything else from us, call my producers."

The officer takes the card as James guides me into the safety of his car.

The three men step closer, and my breath stalls. There's no way they don't see through every lie we tell. They know who I am, and what I've done.

"Is there any way we can get a picture before you leave?" they ask together like a rehearsed choir.

James looks back at me and winks before turning with a smile. After his photoshoot, James joins me in the car.

"You didn't have to do that," I whisper.

James glances my way and shrugs. "I only do things I want to do."

The butterflies in my stomach flutter away as I look towards the future with a hope I may not deserve, but I'm willing to take. Alex is safe, and somehow, I am, too.

29

THE BUTTERFLY EFFECT

BY LINDSAY SCHRAAD KEELING

I was told the flapping of a butterfly's wings has the power to cause a hurricane across the world.

So when a butterfly—with its broken, misshapen wings the color of watered-down iced tea—landed on my palm that summer day on the river, why didn't it stop your lung from collapsing? Why didn't it stop the dementia from eating at your brain like sharks at a carcass in the blue of the ocean? Why didn't it, at the very least, stop the tremors in your hands?

Why didn't it restore your hearing so I could say *I love you* one last time on the phone?

I remembered your words when I called you years ago and you told me, *A phone call from you is worth a million dollars.*

I remembered you grasping my ring finger at the family reunion after I'd gotten engaged, and you said with an ornery grin, *I heard your left hand got a little heavier.*

I remembered the way you asked for God's blessings, our heads collectively bowed low, any time we had a meal at your house.

Instead of you dying, the broken butterfly that landed on my hand that hot day on the river warned me about other things that seem frivolous now: an impending divorce, a three-month-long legal battle with my now ex, navigating the grief of a broken marriage at the age of twenty-five.

Things that mattered at the time seem insignificant when someone you love passes away.

The last thing you told me before the dementia took over was, *Keep your head down,* which I inferred as a long-forgotten memory digging its way out of the depths of your mind, popping up like a mole in a garden, from your Catholic school years. *Keep your head down,* I imagined the nuns saying to you. Most people want you to keep your head up, but I think you were asking me, in your Lewy body-riddled way, to keep praying.

HOOKED UP to wires and an oxygen mask that made his face bloat and swell, my grandfather passed peacefully, surrounded by his wife and three sons at 7:30 PM on a Wednesday evening in July. He'd been hallucinating that he was back at the Oklahoma airport he'd worked at for forty years. Before slipping into a morphine coma, he was making sure the ghosts he envisioned were getting to their flights on time.

When 7:30 PM hit, I was 1,500 miles away in my home in Virginia. Confident I saw the lights in my living room flicker, perhaps it was just a butterfly hitting the bulb.

Somewhere across the ocean, Hurricane Beryl was beginning to dissipate.

30

THE BUTTERFLY'S WINGS

BY KAY DEBORAH LINLEY

Can you hear the butterfly's wings?
Fingertips patting on a deerskin drum
The robin's call?
Familiar drops of light water in the mind
The swallow's chatterbox?
Filling each corner with confidence that life prevails.

I am told freedom is a choice,
so, I reach in
and retrieve this gold
to scatter in all places,
knowing that one microscopic shoot
pushing head above ground
is all it takes

to hear the sacred
drumming.

31

THE SONG OF BUTTERFLIES

BY GERALDINE ANN MARSHALL

Listen, children of the dark-shadowed, comforting mother, of the cool, sheltering father. Listen, Children of the Forest, as the hunt fire smolders, as the camp falls quiet. Hear the story of our ema, our mother, and of Apalura, whose gift woke the Forest. Hear the story of the beings who dance on the breezes, the silent ones who sing to those who listen. Listen, Children of the Forest.

IN THE EARLY TIME, there was Grandmother and there was the Forest and there were the Bambuti, the Children of the Forest.

"Teach our children," whispered the Forest to Grandmother in her dreams, "to hunt antelope and okapi, to gather mushrooms and honey, to build fire and hut. Show the songs and dances that teach about death and tell about living. As I listen to the songs, I will stay awake and give the people food and shelter."

In the day, the children hunted the animals and gathered the fruits of the Forest. In the evening, Grandmother led the songs and dances, and the Forest heard and rejoiced. The Forest stayed awake and took care of the Bambuti.

Into Grandmother's green world, a granddaughter was born. Placed in the wise woman's arms, the child became like a part of her heart. Grandmother sang;

Little bird, little flower,
little Apalura,
brought to me on the breeze,
I shall sing you my songs,
You shall dance like the beat of my heart.

Grandmother created a wonderful blanket for Apalura. The blanket was softer than the finest beaten bark cloth. Its colors were the green of forest trees, the blue of sky glimpsed through the leafy canopy, the orange of fire glow.

As Apalura grew, she played with the other children during the day, but each night, she slept with Grandmother under the wonderful blanket, in their hut of heart-shaped mongongo leaves. Each night, as the blanket held them together in a hug, Apalura asked, "Grandmother, will life always be like this? Will you always teach the songs and lead the dances?"

"Always, you will dance like the beat of my heart. Always, you will hear me singing," Grandmother answered each night.

At last, the day came when Apalura could sing each song without faltering and dance each step without stumbling.

"Grandmother, will life always be like this?" Apalura asked that night. "Will you always teach the songs and lead the dances?" There was no answer but the owl hooting in the night and the mourning coo of the pigeon at dawn.

At first light, Apalura's worst fear came true. She ran from the hut. "Grandmother is dead!"

The Children of the Forest pulled their hair and wept for many days. Then there was a long, lost silence. Grandmother's songs and dances slept in the children's hearts until they forgot the words of the songs and the steps of the dances. Then the Forest slept too, and the children found little to gather and less to hunt. They were hungry.

Apalura stayed by the fire, wrapped in the blanket Grandmother had made for her. She listened for Grandmother's voice but heard only the slow beating of her own heart.

"I cannot hear Grandmother singing in the silence," she cried to herself.

Then, one night, Grandmother visited Apalura in a dream.

"You must wake the Forest," Grandmother whispered.

When the pigeon cooed, Apalura left her hut, and traveled through the Forest. She took only the blanket, her gift from Grandmother.

At last, Apalura paused by the Ituri River. She splashed across to a small island of sand. Then, though her heart ached, she sang:

I will remember you
in the birds, in the flowers,
in the breezes that caress.
I shall sing into the silence.
I will be with you with each beat of my heart.

The Forest heard Apalura's song and woke to smile once again on the Children of the Forest. Apalura swirled the blanket around her. It fell beneath her dancing feet. From the place where it hit the ground there rose many bright beings. These beings had wings that shone with the green of forest trees, the blue of sky glimpsed through the forest canopy, the orange of fire glow. They danced on breezes between earth and sky. They sang a silent song heard only by the hearts of those who listen.

Apalura returned to the Children of the Forest to teach them again the songs and dances of death and of living. The Children named the bright beings after her. So, in the Bambuti language, *apalura* means *butterflies*.

And, always after that, Apalura heard Grandmother singing in her heart and felt the forest breezes holding her in a hug.

Editors Note

THE BAMBUTI: THE FOREST'S CHILDREN

Imagine living in a world where you travel from camp to camp, living in beehive-shaped huts made of branches and leaves, huts just big enough to lie down in.

Imagine living in a world in which your food is what can be found in the African rainforest. You eat antelope, okapi and hyrax meat. For a nice change, you sometimes eat fungus and termites. And occasionally—when someone has climbed more than 100 feet into a tall tree pulling a basket on a vine rope—you eat some of the forest's best gift, honey.

Imagine that people have lived there in much the same way for more than 4,000 years.

This world really exists, for it is the world of the Bambuti, who live in the Democratic Republic of the Congo (formerly known as Zaire), in Africa. In about 2,250 BC, when an Egyptian Pharaoh wrote a description of a "dancing dwarf of the god from the land of spirits," he was describing someone from the Bambuti people. Many call the Bambuti pygmies, from a Greek word meaning the distance between an ancient Greek man's elbow and his knuckles. Though the Bambuti are not that small, they are the smallest people in the world: grown-up men and women are about four and a half feet tall, and sometimes even shorter.

The Bambuti think of the forest as a loving parent who provides everything they need to live. If something bad happens, they believe it is because the forest is sleeping, and they sing to wake the forest. My story, "The Song of Butterflies," is based on their traditions and tells of the first time the forest needed to be woken up.

The modern world is beginning to change the Bambuti way of life. They are settling into permanent villages, and much of their forest home is being taken away from them. Perhaps we can hope that, before it is too late, the Bambuti can teach the rest of us how to love the forest as our mother and father and how we too can sing as children of the forest.

32

KESIA'S MUSICAL GARDEN

BY GENEVIÈVE LAPRISE

Kesia's eyes fluttered open. She lay in a hospital bed surrounded by grey, peeling walls. On either side were cold, metal bedrails. Bruises coloured her frail left arm, a butterfly IV port in her hand, and on her right was a useless, empty old chair. Every day was the same, and today would be no different. The same pain, the same nurses doing the same thing, the same cancer, eating away at her. No one would visit her; she was alone. She peered out the window at a grey sky and the branches of a dying tree.

Everything ends, she thought as she watched the branches reaching out to her window. Sighing, Kesia moved her gaze back to the grey ceiling of her hospital room.

The machinery beside her whirred quietly. In the hall, people sobbed and moaned, comforting their loved ones with hushed voices. There would be no comfort for her. The girl shivered under a white sheet. Pushing herself up, she gripped the knitted lavender blanket her mother had made for her long ago. Kesia lay, wrapped in melancholy, when quiet footsteps in the hall stopped near her room.

"The girl in room 415 is almost gone. We'll move Mr George up here in a day or two. I think Mrs Carson will be in room 405 before the end of the day."

Kesia slumped back in her bed and closed her eyes. She had no more tears to cry, yet she longed for someone to care. They used to call her Kesia and talk to her, but for the past few weeks, they referred to her as the girl. A black-haired nurse in a starched white uniform walked into her room and adjusted her IV, eyes fixed on her work. The intercom pinged, and the nurse listened to the message.

"Attention. Code Blue in room 405."

Another soul lost.

After a short pause, a new ping announced a second message.

"Code Blue cancelled."

An end to the pain.

The nurse continued her morning routine. Down the corridor, an unusual and familiar sound emerged. Kesia sat up straighter and cocked her head to listen. Someone played a piano. Her heart rate accelerated, and the corners of her lips curled into a smile. The notes were slow and measured at first. Soon, they faltered and became discordant, filled with pain as disease tore through the pianist's life without mercy. Despair ensued until the song burst into a sudden jubilation. Oh, how she longed to play one last time. The nurse glanced at the smiling girl. After a long moment, the music stopped, and the nurse left.

Soon, the woman returned with a wheelchair and transferred Kesia into it. Where were they going? She stared at the peeling white paint as the nurse rolled her down the hall to a community room. A young man and woman lounged on a ripped, grey couch, hugging each other and sobbing. An old woman, pale and frail, attached to an IV, sat on the wooden rocking chair staring at a world she longed to rejoin. An elderly man on another couch smiled weakly at Kesia when she entered. Some of these people were ill, some healthy but grief-stricken, and some were slowly dying. There was no joy or peace here, only sadness, before the music came.

This room wasn't new to Kesia, but the piano had never been there before. The instrument called to her with its sparkling lacquer and beautifully polished surface. It infused her failing body with energy and hope. A quiet excitement pushed forward, her hands gripping the armrests of the wheelchair. When the nurse engaged the brakes after stopping next to the piano bench, Kesia scooted forward, her energy renewed for a moment.

An orderly helped transfer her onto the white wooden bench as the nurse moved the IV stand next to her and adjusted the line.

Kesia grinned and inhaled deeply, straightened her back, and poised her hands above the keys. With a slow, measured exhale, she let her long, delicate fingers glide over the keys, releasing wondrous music into the bleak world. With every touch of the piano, her pain faded and her heart rejoiced. She hadn't felt this alive and happy in months. With every note, colourful light painted the drab room into a work of abstract art. Every luminescent wisp was a dancing soul who found peace through music, which would lead her to her own happiness.

She ignored the sheet music; she wasn't performing "Claire de Lune" anyway. Instead, she played the song of her heart, releasing the pain, fear, and loss into wisps of colourful, joyous light dancing around her. The beauty was mesmerising, and the tune frantic but also measured, like her emotions. The music gave her a quiet strength, just enough to play one last time, and that broke her heart. Music was everything to her, and her disease couldn't take it away, not yet, not ever.

Kesia's fingers ached, but her smile grew as she played; the pain a distant memory. The magical colours intensified and swirled to the enchanting music she had created with her hands and soul. The world continued to turn without her, and she didn't mind at all.

People gathered around, some healthy, some in their final moments, pushed in by nurses. Doctors stopped in front of the door to listen, but Kesia paid them no mind. An ill man muttered something about a blue butterfly in her ear.

The stormy colours of their feelings melded with her music, threatening to overpower her magic, but she refused to let the darkness, the pain, and the despair touch her.

This was no longer her world. Hers would be one of imagination, beauty, and soul.

The music told her story. It was her art, her escape. The people trapped in this life had suffered as much or maybe more than she had. They understood the music but couldn't see the magic unfold before them.

No thoughts, no pain, only music, she reminded herself.

The melody became discordant as her focus wavered. The colours bled into each other. She shifted slightly on the bench and breathed deeply, staring at the now yellow, orange, and green wall before her.

"Let your fingers speak for you; guide you. Let the music take you to a wonderful land where there is only joy and beauty. Don't think; just move your fingers and let your heart show you the way," her mother had said.

The memory of her mother's words sent a pang of grief

through her, but grounded her focus. She slowed the rhythm into a melancholic hymn.

A soft smile curled her lips as tiny colourful butterflies came to life, fluttering around her and the piano. She watched them dance, content but unaware of their charm. Her fingers slowed, but the music continued. Her gaze followed the blue butterfly perched on the tip of her nose—her mother used to touch the tip of her nose every morning when she woke up. She could almost feel her standing beside the bench. Oh, how she missed her mother. She would do anything to have one more day with her. Kesia had taken those moments for granted, not knowing her mother would soon be gone. Those were her most precious memories.

"Good morning, sweetheart. I hope you slept well. The world is yours today. Time to get up."

The blue butterfly fluttered away, joining the others. She wanted to follow them and dance with them, but alas, she remained tethered to this grey world.

She sighed as her mother spoke again.

"Your music is magic, Sweetheart. It's so beautiful. It takes all the pain away."

Her heart swelled with pride and happiness, bringing tears to her eyes. Her fingers glided over the keys, and the music filled her soul with glee and peace.

The colours swirled before her. Kesia became light-headed. Her eyelids drooped, and she sighed as her pulse slowed. The music played, and her eyes fluttered open once more. She stood from her bench with ease. Kesia stepped forward, following the blue butterfly through the myriad of colours. A smile, a genuine, painless smile, tugged at the corners of her lips as she walked through the dancing colours, leaving her diseased body behind. The music followed her; it encouraged her forward, away from the pain to a magical, musical tranquillity.

The cold she had felt for months in the hospital dissipated, replaced by a comforting, warm breeze that smelled of lavender and roses. The colours shifted and grew wings of beauty. She watched in awe as they fluttered by on the music of her heart, moving through the emptiness before her. The colourful butterflies settled upon the ground, giving birth to tall, lush trees, grass, and flowers.

The music continued to play in the afterlife, as Kesia glanced at the wonders growing across her paradise. She wiggled her toes in the grass and inhaled deeply. She had almost forgotten what nature felt and smelled like. The darkness had receded, and in its place, a garden filled with light and life blossomed. She spun with her arms wide, eyes on the blue, cloudless sky, feeling the warmth of the breeze on her face. She giggled as she twirled, not a worry in the world.

Soft laughter caught her attention. As the music slowed and faded, Kesia stopped, searching for the familiar, melodious sound. She knew that laugh well, but hadn't heard it in so long. Her heart skipped a beat as she spun to find the woman of her memories, not as she was in her last, dying moments, but as she was before death took her youth, her voice, her music, and finally, her life.

The woman with bright ginger hair, fox-like grey eyes, a contagious smile, and a heart filled with love smiled and spread her arms wide. Kesia gasped. She hopped once and ran over to her mother. The scent of freshly baked cookies filled her with joyous memories as she embraced her mother. They hugged for a long moment before the girl found her voice.

"Mama! You're here!"

Her mother caressed her hair and held her tightly. "Welcome to your garden, sweetheart. I missed you so much."

Kesia's heart burst with bliss as tears swelled in her eyes. "I missed you too, Mama."

Kesia's mother released her and studied her features for a long moment. Then, she touched the tip of her nose with a genuine smile.

"Come with me. I want to show you something."

Kesia's mother turned, wrapping an arm around her daughter's shoulders as they strolled barefoot in the vibrant, verdant garden.

Soon, they came upon a fountain surrounded by a stone path. Butterflies fluttered from flower to flower as the water trickled into a basin. A bench sat facing the marble statue of an angel; her hands cupped in front of her. A small, white rabbit hopped about in the garden, stopping to eat clovers.

"It's like Alice in Wonderland," Kesia said, watching the bunny eat.

"It's all yours. Thank you for sharing it with me," her mother said, smiling.

"What else is here?"

"Whatever you want. You created this place. It's your paradise."

"Really?"

"Yes, really. You deserve it."

"It's amazing," she exclaimed, soaking in every detail, bending down to smell a pink flower. A butterfly soared into the air and danced around her. Kesia smiled. Her mother took her hand and gently pulled her forward.

As Kesia rounded the fountain, she reached out to the water. The warm liquid flowed between her fingers. Cupping her hands, she gathered water and drank. The soothing liquid slid gently down her throat. Kesia followed her mother past a well-manicured hedge to a majestic, white grand piano. The girl clapped and grinned, bouncing in place. She rushed to the piano and sat on the pearlized bench, her smile wide. It was the grandest of pianos she had ever seen; a real dream come true. Glancing back at her mother, she tapped the seat next to her. Her mother smiled and walked forth, sitting beside Kesia. All was as it should be.

Kesia touched the key, and the note reverberated through her garden. The butterflies took flight as she played the song of her soul. Kesia's mother brushed a strand of hair behind her ear and joined her daughter. Their fingers moved effortlessly over the keys. They played together, as they used to. The colourful butterflies danced as Kesia's new life began in her musical garden.

33

THE BUTTERFLY GARDEN

BY PINES CALLAHAN

It's hard to consider the loftiness of souls with my hands in the earth. Grounded by soil and sweat, the last thing I wanted while laboring in the hot soup we called a summer was to be asked my opinion on an afterlife. "I try not to dwell on the big stuff, ma'am."

Mrs. Wallace smiled widely, showing teeth too flawless and white to be anything but dentures. "Of course. Here I am, talking your ear off and slowing you down when you're doing all this as a favor. Where are my manners?"

"Your manners are fine, and Chris wouldn't have passed Algebra without you paying extra attention. I owed you one."

Her wrist cracked loudly as she waved off my thanks. "Oh, bless your heart, you didn't owe me anything. He brought his grade up because he put in the work."

It was true, but I'd never allow the grand old girl to feel like a charity case. She was too proud for that. Mrs. Wallace offered me a lemonade that tasted fresh from the massive tree in her front yard, tart and invigorating. I took a long swig as we watched a Monarch open and shut her wings on a scrawny milkweed. She touched her back end to a leaf and laid an egg. Her future offspring needed ten or so full leaves before making a chrysalis; the plant's four total would guarantee starvation. I'd need to install one of the hearty, thick-stemmed replacement plants close enough that the caterpillar could crawl its way to a decent meal.

"Cathy loved butterflies, you know," Mrs. Wallace told me for the fifth time. Her daughter had been gone for twenty years. "Whenever there's butterflies around, I know she's here with me, and there are *always* butterflies around. Have you ever heard of anything like that before?"

I accepted a still-warm blueberry muffin she offered off a tray shaped like a teddy bear and took a massive bite instead of answering. Call me skeptical. We lived in the tropics, and she regularly told my kids how much she loved to garden. Butterflies seemed more like cause and effect than supernatural intervention. I'd spent years working with pollinator plants and had never seen the insects act like anything other than, well, bugs. The few flitting around weren't behaving out of the ordinary here, either. A big, lemon-colored Cloudless Sulphur bounced along my hat and loitered on the brim for a few seconds before flying away. Not shocking, I smelled like flowers.

Chewing slowly, I searched the bones of what was obviously once a lush, well-planned butterfly habitat for something worthy of a topic change. Dead vines, weeds, and corpses of shrubs. I hadn't missed the thickness in Mrs. Wallace's knuckles, the shake of her hands, or the way she was already sweating more than my glass of lemonade. Nothing I could point out would be news to a woman who watched her space decay as her body made a favorite hobby inaccessible. It was the elderly gardener's curse.

I could swallow or chew the muffin like cud, so I

emptied my mouth. "You know, I can't say that I've seen anything like that before, but it sure would be a wonder."

She beamed like I was Santa at Christmas. "A wonder indeed. It's a bit hot out here for me, though. I'll check in on you later. Give me a holler if you'd like another drink."

Slowly, and wincing at the movement, she turned on her heels and went back inside. A Monarch circled her lazily for a moment, orbiting around her silver head like a halo, before investigating the clump of plants I'd unloaded on the far side of the garden. I downed the rest of my lemonade and got back to work.

One of the best things about revamping old gardens was finding hidden gems that could be coaxed back towards health with some compost, fish emulsion, and a heavy prune. There was plenty worth saving, more than I'd expected when I picked out replacement plants. At one point, Mrs. Wallace had clearly known her stuff, but the garden's hidden success slowed my progress. Every host plant I touched was already occupied by caterpillars or chrysalis. I snipped the branches ornamented with butterflies-in-waiting and hung them in a line along Mrs. Wallace's fence post. I'd read somewhere that butterflies retained memories from their caterpillarhood despite spending time as goo in a sack; I wondered what the newly emerged butterflies would think of their change in scenery.

Later, Mrs. Wallace offered me lunch, and we ate in her airy, lemon-scented kitchen while she told me about her heart troubles and complained that her two remaining kids in Ontario never called. She wiped her eyes and sniffed a little. "Cathy lived right down the street. We planted the original garden here together. You would have loved her."

"If she had anything to do with that garden, I bet you're right."

Mrs. Wallace's eyes shone as she looked through her big bay window. "We designed it together. There's always been a little bit of her soul here."

After lunch, there were half a dozen butterflies dancing over the freshly bare dirt. Like they were waiting for me to plant something. The thought was silly, but the first Privet Cassia shrub I placed had ten or so butterflies drinking off its yellow popcorn flowers within minutes. "You guys sure knew where the party was going to be."

I planted two more Privet Cassia for the Sulphurs, then a Grayleaf Teabush with silvery foliage and baby-pink blossoms. Next came Goldenrods, whose flower spikes would grow as tall as me, and lavender-spired Blazing Stars to complement it. Coreopsis, White Tropical Sage, Black-Eyed Susans, and Beach Verbena filled out the wildflowers. Clusters of lacy Frogfruit, more purple Porterweed, and Suessian-bloomed pink Sunshine Mimosa would spread like wildfire and ward off less-desirable invaders trying to take over the mostly sunny space. Blue-flowered Creeping Sage would fill in the shady corners and host Fulvous Hairstreak butterflies. Finally, three different kinds of native milkweed for the Monarchs. As I wrapped up, the number of butterflies had swelled to several dozen. I got the impression I was being watched, but the garden was empty and Mrs. Wallace wasn't visible in her kitchen. The hair on the back of my neck stood on end. I rubbed it down with a gloved hand, spreading dirt over sun-sensitive skin.

"Have another lemonade, sugar," Mrs. Wallace said from behind me, sending me into the air like one of her winged visitors. She watched the fluttering garden with a soft smile, stretching the drink out towards me. Her arm wobbled.

I took the glass from her. "Lots of butterflies already. They were waiting for this."

Mrs. Wallace nodded. "It's Cathy. She's here for me."

What kind of jerk would I have been to argue with her? "I can't remember the last time I saw this many butterflies at once. There's definitely something special going on."

She dipped her head solemnly, and a tear rolled down her creased cheek. "I knew you'd understand."

"I'm glad I could help you out." I powered through half the lemonade and set it on her patio table. "I'm pretty much done here, I'll come back tomorrow with a load of mulch."

"This was so kind of you. I'll never forget your generosity. Neither will Cathy."

I didn't know what to say to that, so I nodded and packed up my things. She wobbled over to a stone bench under a white-flowered Chaste Tree. Her knees crackled like bubble wrap as she sat, wincing.

"You ok, Mrs. Wallace?"

"I'm fine. I think I'll sit here for a little while, enjoy my new plants."

"All right, I'm heading out. I'll see you tomorrow."

She hummed agreeably and closed her eyes.

About half way home, I realized I'd left my good weeding knife under a half-dead passionvine. There were dark clouds overhead, and I hated leaving my tools in the rain. A few minutes later, I was back in Mrs. Wallace's garden. I passed the fence where I'd hung the chrysalis and stopped mid-stride. All two dozen were empty, and fresh butterflies hung off the remains. I pulled out my phone to take a picture, but Mrs. Wallace caught my eye.

She was still sitting on the bench under the Chaste tree, but slumped sideways like a ragdoll. Her eyes were open but unfocused, and her mouth hung slack. Even at a distance, I could tell she was gone. A huge, freshly emerged Monarch perched on her lips, slowly opening and shutting wings still folded and heavy from emerging.

I rushed towards her, body moving on autopilot as I tried to process the fact that the soul I'd shared lemonade with an hour earlier was gone, but the largest Monarch I'd ever seen, nearly the size of my palm, flapped into my path at face level. I swatted at it, but four more flew to its defense. In seconds, a flurry of at least ten different species surrounded me. The butterflies spiraled around me like a school of fish. I could make out Mrs. Wallace behind them. The butterfly on her lips beat its wings impossibly fast to dry them and raised itself into the air. The wall of butterflies blocking me turned like a flock of birds and joined it above the dead woman. They all swooped around the garden for a few seconds, then lifted into the sky and scattered in an explosion of color.

Much as it embarasses me to admit, I ran back to my truck faster than I'd moved since track and field. I white-knuckled it the whole way home, barely keeping myself at five over the speed limit. My wife asked me if I'd seen a ghost as I stumbled into the living room, half drunk from fear. I nearly broke down telling her what happened. She got teary-eyed and said it was Cathy, come to collect her mother. I wanted to argue in favor of logic, but there was no logical explanation for what I'd witnessed. I drifted back to Shakespeare in freshman English: maybe there were more things in heaven and earth than I'd dreamt of in my philosophy. What else was out there that I'd never considered? Bugs and a dead woman were pushing me head-first into an existential crisis.

The dead woman. "I left the old girl in her garden, and I didn't even call anyone. I have to go back." I'd never wanted to do anything less in my life, but I couldn't stand the thought of Mrs. Wallace sitting out there alone, slumped on her bench.

She was right where the butterflies and I had left her. I called 911 and let them know she was past the point of help. I mentioned her heart troubles but left out the rest. My chest ached as I hung up the phone. Uncanniness aside, Mrs. Wallace had been a lovely person, and I'd been the one to give her the last help she'd ever receive. It felt like an honor, and an obligation to her memory. To Cathy's memory. To whatever the hell weirdness was happening in the garden.

The swarm of thousands was gone, but there were still nearly a hundred butterflies busying themselves around her garden. Two female Monarchs hovered at eye level. The big ones. They kept their distance while I tidied a few things and waited for the ambulance, dancing with each other between the new plants. The smaller, fresher Monarch landed on the rim of the lemonade I'd left on Mrs. Wallace's patio table. I half expected it to offer me another glass.

Something caught my eye on the ground next to her Chaste tree. A notebook. I flipped through a few rough sketches of flowers, but stopped to study Mrs. Wallace's last picture. It was her, squeezed inside a chrysalis. A butterfly with a woman's face hovered over Mrs. Wallace's head. Cathy. I closed my eyes against the sting of tears and imagined the soul-altering pain birthed by the loss of a child. How dim the flowers must have looked with her garden helper gone. I'd cling to whatever hope I could that we'd be together again someday, too. Who was I to say what form that hope and the bond between a mother and daughter could take? Who knew how much we could change ourselves for love?

They say a soul weighs twenty-one grams. The average

Monarch weighs half a gram. It would take nearly a hundred butterflies to equal the weight of two human souls. My arms broke out in goosebumps.

I opened my eyes again and set the notebook down next to what was left of Mrs. Wallace's human chrysalis. Two Monarchs circled me, watching. The reflection of ambulance lights sparkled off my glass of watered-down lemonade. Hopefully, I could make a quick statement to the paramedics and go home for a stiffer drink.

"I'll bring y'all a drip hose on a timer when I spread the mulch. Don't want your new plants going thirsty." I lifted my hat to the butterflies as they swirled. "Ladies."

34

BUTTERFLY'S KISS

BY NATHANIEL MENDOZA AND
DR. LESTER N. LINSANGAN

Somewhere in Heaven, I run,
touched and kissed by the sun,
as fields of flowers like daffodils,
love and peace my heart only feels.

Linger the grass so aesthetic,
to live like me is romantic,
I flew around the colorful rainbows,
kaleidoscopes are my shadows.

Ocean paints the clouds and sky,
I'm a teal-colored, pretty butterfly,
Midnights have my morning show,
twilight's the shade of my wings' glow.

I leap and dance through the air,
found the beauty of life that is rare,
to fly around the world it is,
to adore someone that you truly miss.

35

BATESIA HYPOCHLORA

BY MORGAN MATLOW

The day my mom died, so did all her butterflies. In her entire butterfly garden of over fifty, all that survived was one little caterpillar.

Mom used to go into that garden every day, nurturing her large assortment of flowers and herbs, an entire rainbow of plants. All so her butterflies would never leave. When I was young, she'd take me out to that garden and show me all the different kinds of butterflies, each more vibrant and beautiful than the last. But I've always identified more with the moths—duller, nocturnal, and stocky in comparison to their bright, sunny counterparts.

I wake up at 2 P.M. today, groggy as ever, and shuffle straight for the coffee maker. While Mom always made her tea from herbs in her garden with a large dollop of honey, I take my coffee black, drinking it only for the energy to get me through my night shift. My hand hovers briefly over the canister of tea Mom made for me a month before she died. I've never even touched it. Considering it for the briefest moment, I know having tea instead of my usual coffee would not be a good idea. Who knows what tea could do to me when my body runs on brown sludge.

Sentimentality that leads me to a sleepy night could get me fired.

Fatal sentimentality somehow doesn't stop me from packing up the caterpillar in my bag when I leave for work. I made him an enclosure, a jar just caterpillar sized, so he wouldn't get smooshed or thrown around. He's my responsibility now. His mom's gone and so is mine. There's no one left to look after the little guy.

"Hey, Perkins," the guard greets me as I pull up to the barbed wire fence. I give a stiff smile in response, a signal to just let me go on past. I'm not up for chit chat tonight. He buzzes me through, and I find the parking spot farthest from the building. I always need the extra steps.

There's a chill to the night air. Good. It means Fall is on the way. Maybe all the butterflies died because of the cold, not because of a broken heart.

How heartless would I be in comparison? To just keep living, soulless and unfeeling.

My office is gray. No better way to put it. Gray walls, gray chair, gray desk. No decorations or pictures. Just twelve screens, each for a different part of the building I'm supposed to monitor.

I take the caterpillar from my bag, noticing he still hangs from the stick I put in there for him, two thin transparent strands holding his upper body to the stick. I place the jar on my desk, happy to have him there, but knowing my full focus needs to be on the monitors.

It's only a moment later when I glance at him again, and his body has changed. It's still green, but it's bigger now, and he seems to have shed some skin. Is it a chrysalis? He was still a caterpillar only a few minutes ago. Did he really transform so fast? An internet search tells me that caterpillars do change into their chrysalises quickly, but more like over the span of an hour. Not a matter of minutes.

My search also tells me that this is the most delicate stage of the process; any wrong move could hurt the exoskeleton. I'll need to keep a watchful eye. It should take over a week before it comes out of the chrysalis transformed. I wish *I* could be fully transformed in a week. It would be nice to transfigure my mental health and make me a happier, better person all in the span of ten days.

When I get up to grab a bottle of water from the fridge, something crashes behind me. I turn back to my desk, remembering how delicate the caterpillar is in this first part of the cocoon stage. The jar lays in pieces on the ground.

My pulse races as panic sets in. I thought I'd left the jar sturdy on my desk. Had I pushed it toward the edge when I stood up? Had there been a heavy draft that knocked it down? Clearly this is all my fault. But the caterpillar has to be here somewhere.

I rush to sift through the pieces, hoping to save my caterpillar friend. He can't be gone. I'm not sure I could handle the implications. But there's no green lump in the wreckage. Instead, something brushes my head. Once, twice, three times. I bring my hand up to brush whatever it is away as I search under my desk for the caterpillar. I just need to know if he's still alive.

With no sign of my little caterpillar under the desk, I shift back out and into a sitting position. My heart sinks. The last piece I had of Mom is gone.

Something brushes my head again, and I reach up to bat it away for a fifth time. But when I look at it, there flutters a bright pink and yellow butterfly, intricate swirls painted on its wings. I don't think I've ever seen one quite like this.

It couldn't be my caterpillar, could it? But in this sealed office, there's no way it could have gotten in.

How could it have transformed so quickly? Within the space of less than an hour from caterpillar to cocoon to butterfly.

"You're not supposed to be in here," I say, taking a swat at the caterpillar-turned-butterfly, narrowly missing it by just a centimeter. "Come here!"

If I don't catch it, I could get in serious trouble. We aren't supposed to have any sort of a distraction in here, let alone a live animal. When it was just a boring caterpillar, it was one thing. But now that it's a fully-grown, flying bug, it poses a threat. I really don't want to kill it. That's the last thing Mom would want.

I was seven when Mom first brought me to her butterfly garden. She showed me all the best plants to attract the butterflies. Her collection held milkweed, sage, mint, and even squash.

"Squash isn't a flower," I said to her with a giggle.

She plucked one of the blossoms for me with her purple-gloved hand, then held it out for me to smell.

"Many plants bloom, even if that isn't what we use them for. Orange trees blossom too, and their flowers are so pretty."

"Blossom?" I said.

"Blossoms come with the spring, often flowers on the plants we might not even harvest until summer or fall. Sometimes things take a little longer to blossom, but they develop beautifully when they eventually do come."

I just nodded, trying to wrap my little brain around how so many things could blossom.

"And, one day," Mom said, "you'll blossom too. You'll find your personality and knowledge of the world, and you'll be in full bloom."

I don't feel like I've ever quite been in full bloom.

The butterfly lands on top of one of my monitors, flapping its wings slowly, giving me gorgeous views of the intricate pink and yellow design. I inch toward it, unable to decide what to do if I catch the thing. I don't know if I have the heart to kill it. I know by work's standard, it's what I should do. Get rid of the thing distracting me.

This is the last remaining caterpillar—butterfly—Mom ever welcomed in her garden.

Each year, at the beginning of Spring, Mom would put out whatever she could to bring the butterflies in. She cultivated bigger and better gardens every year to attract them. They probably would have returned regardless. Why not come back to the lady who plants pretty flowers and leaves you all the nectar and sap you could eat?

Granted, there was once a time where I thought I might not return home in the Spring either. My freshman year of college, I thought I had it all figured out. I moved three states away, where I got an apartment and a job. I might have stayed there forever. It would have just been Mom and her butterflies.

But I eventually came back, too. After one of the roughest years I have ever had, which had nothing to do with school, and had everything to do with being unprepared for the world ahead of me, I came back to her.

And she was as sweet as could be. She forgave me for every cross word I had spat at her when she warned me of dating a guy ten years older than me at eighteen. And for moving in with him and paying his rent. She never said, '*I told you so*' or asked for any penance for my mistakes. She just made me a cup of tea with a large dollop of honey and helped me find a new job.

I later asked her why she had been so kind to me after, and all she said was, "it wasn't going to fix anything. And when you went off, I knew you had some blossoming to do, and you had to do it on your own."

And that was that.

"Come on," I say to the butterfly after another swat at him. I've commandeered an old water bottle to put him in, planning to open the straw once I've caught him so he has plenty of air. But it's not big enough for him to escape again.

I'll stop by Mom's on the way home and release him into the garden. Hopefully, he will learn quickly to not keep coming back. Because she isn't there anymore.

I slump into my chair, my chest rising and sinking with heavy breaths. The screens in front of me show all the rooms I'm monitoring are empty and have had no activity. Good. Sometimes, it feels like my job is pointless. I just sit here and stare at screens, every once in a while stepping out of the office to check out something weird.

I wasn't able to finish college, but Mom never made me feel bad for that. She always said I would figure out what I was meant to do eventually. That my job didn't determine my worth. Despite this, I've always felt a little like I was behind. All my friends were growing beyond my limits. Careers brought them to places far away, and starting families meant they outgrew me, too.

"Your time will come," Mom would always say. But without her here to tell me, I'm not sure if I could ever believe it. With her gone, I'm on an island, doing the same boring job day after day and amounting to nothing.

The butterfly stares at me from his new perch, sitting on top of my fridge next to a picture of Mom and me that Dad took before he passed away when I was ten. Mom always said it was her favorite because it was through Dad's eyes, so we'd always have a view of how he saw us. The little girl staring back at me isn't the same girl I am today. She had pink and yellow butterfly clips in her hair. I have only dark dead ends and bags under my eyes.

When I asked Mom how she did everything without Dad, she told me she had to live each day for both of them. She would create moments he would have wanted to experience. For this reason, she would always get a second ice cream cup when we went out. She always placed an extra seat for him in the garden. And without a doubt, she would always ride his favorite roller coaster when we went to amusement parks even though she hated them. Just because Dad would have done it. She never wanted him to miss a moment. She never wanted me to, either.

It's nearly 3 A.M. when I lose sight of the butterfly completely. Because of the extra energy I exerted that evening, I fall asleep in my chair for only a few moments, and when I wake up, my butterfly friend is missing. Not on top of a monitor or the fridge. I look under the desk and even in the drawers for the creature, catching a few sneezes with how much dust I inhale.

Despite the insect murder I had contemplated earlier in the night, I miss him. Because, if there is one thing he gave me in this game of chase, it was the most entertaining shift I have had in years. I haven't had something this exciting since someone broke in to kiss the elephant statue after dark.

So, I continue my search for him, almost crushing him when I find him sitting in my bag atop of the book I brought for light reading on the slow nights. Okay, every night. More specifically, Butterfly is sitting on the bookmark.

I slide the book from my bag gingerly, careful not to brush Butterfly's wings on anything. He refuses to move from the bookmark, so I extricate it from the book, noticing how his feet grasp onto the edge.

Mom gave me this bookmark when I told her I wanted to start reading more. On one side, it says, *Don't be afraid to spread your wings.* On the other, it has a picture of a monarch butterfly. Butterfly spreads his wings slowly as if to demonstrate.

"Thanks for the reminder," I say.

A laugh escapes me. First, this thing completely develops in one night, and now, he's trying to communicate with me.

When Mom gave me this bookmark, she probably never meant for it to be the only one I'd ever use. At the only job I'd ever have. I'm sure she intended for me to eventually get out of here and do something with my life. The day before she died, she gave me a brochure for summer coding programs I could take. Quick and easy. I could do them at my own pace. She even suggested I do them while working.

"That's frowned upon," I said.

"The only person around at night to stop you is yourself," she said. "And, I'm noticing, Spencer, you never said it wasn't something you're interested in. I think you'd be great at coding."

She never looked down on me for not going back to college, but she never stopped trying to help me grow beyond my place here as a security officer.

And maybe she was right, maybe I would like coding. But the conversation stopped there. Because no matter what hopes she had for me, they died with her. There was no more living for Dad. There was no more living for me for that matter, either. Because the queen of the butterflies died, leaving her littlest caterpillar all alone.

I bring the water bottle close to the bookmark, attempting to slide the butterfly into the bottle with ease. But, of course, just as I touch the edge of the water bottle to the bookmark, Butterfly springs from the edge of it, taking flight around the room again.

This thing is going to get me *so* fired. They will come in about an hour to replace me, and I will still be chasing him down.

Butterfly stares at me from the very top monitor, wiggling one of his antennas in a taunt. He's so lucky I don't want to damage any of this expensive equipment. I find the page in my book, placing the bookmark back in it, and slide the book back into the bag. But not before catching sight of something bright yellow and pink at the bottom.

I pull out the crinkled and slightly smushed brochure, big block letters in yellow and pink advertising the coding program. Did Mom put this here? I had left it on her counter the day she tried to give it to me. I had decided I wasn't going to try.

She must have put it there. How else would it get there? Butterfly brandishes his wings slowly at me, flashing me the same pink and yellow from the brochure.

A tear falls onto the brochure. It's then I notice the stinging that only comes from crying.

Why did she have to go? The only person who believed in me and loved me in this world?

When I look at Butterfly again, his wing flaps seem to say, *Time to live life for her too.* And I know he's right. She lived life for me for so long. Had the patience with me I couldn't have with myself. She always looked out for me. She never failed to bring me back to myself in the worst moments. And she isn't here to do it now, in the worst moment.

So, I have to do it for myself.

My four o'clock alarm goes off, signaling the end of work. The morning shift will be here soon, and the office is a mess.

I hurry to tidy the office, putting everything back into its place so the morning shift won't think I've completely lost my mind. Maybe I have. After all, I watched a caterpillar transform into a butterfly overnight to help me with grieving my late mother.

It's in the moment I pack up my bag that I worry how I will catch Butterfly.

"You can't stay in here," I tell him, but he just wiggles his antennas in response. "Get down here, Silly." With a few slow flaps of his wings, he lands gracefully on my shoulder.

We walk out of there together, and I know Butterfly won't fly away. Even if he does, he'll always find his way back to my shoulder.

And, as I sit in Mom's garden, tending it for her, planting the mint and squash, Butterfly is right there with me. When hundreds of new butterflies grace the garden, Butterfly comes with them.

Of course, there comes a day when Butterfly doesn't fly in with the others. Butterflies don't live that long. But I imagine that he just found his way to Mom's new butterfly garden, wherever she's found herself in the afterlife. Her, and all the other butterflies that ever visited her in life.

And, when I start my new coding job, just over a year later, I get to sit in the garden on a lazy Sunday afternoon, just like Mom always did. I have to live life for two now. For me and for Mom.

Every once in a while, a moth or two finds their way into

the butterfly garden at night, but I've long since realized I'm not like them. I was more like the caterpillar, green and unassuming. In need of guidance. But now, I'm not that caterpillar anymore. I've undergone metamorphosis, becoming something entirely new—all thanks to the last of Mom's butterflies.

36

LEARNING TO FLY

BY NATALIE NEE

The sun will continue its cruel burn, the moon its midnight frolic. The distance grows with each shovelful of dirt, every tick of a clock's hand. A future you thought you'd have evaporates with the morning dew and a new, fragile life is born—shelled in shock and pain and *how will I go on without you*?

So starts the timeline: before and after. The next stage of forgoing food, isolation, and turning your world upside down comes second nature. Weave yourself in silks of black, disintegrate every tissue, and let the world carry on with its endless bustle.

Once you emerge, you'll stretch those unfamiliar wings, but feel that same whisper of wind, the same caress of dawn. Flight will be aimless and haphazard at first, especially when gliding over your childhood home, or breezing past that lakeside Vietnamese restaurant you frequented together every summer and they ask where you are. You'll flit between the blue-spurred columbine and violet-kissed asters along those cherished mountain trails, past the plum-laden trees they planted when your children were born, remembering the appetite you once had for life.

Ever so slowly, your wings will grow stronger. You'll soon waltz and pirouette through your garden, bathing in the fragrant blooms that remain. Though I'd gladly slither and slink through this world if it meant you were by my side, I continue my flight, if only because you'd want to see me soar.

37

BUTTERFLY NET

BY REBECCA LINAM

The story you are about to read is true. The names have been changed to protect the innocent.

This is the village—Wildwood, Alabama, population 1253. It's a hodgepodge of small 1950s-style houses, retired gardeners, and a handful of mom-and-pop stores. Most of the families have lived here for generations. People mind their own business for the most part, but when crime rears its head, I go to work; I carry a badge.

On Monday morning, the weather was cool and sunny, ripe for gardening. My partner, Bob Cannon, and I were working the day watch out at the police office when the call came in. Mrs. Gladys Sanders reported something about stolen property. She was upset and wanted us to come immediately. Bob picked me up in the car at the front of the station.

"So, Jim, another day of big crime in the small city, eh?" He turned left onto Main Street and stopped at a crosswalk with three old men.

"Haha," I replied with a roll of my eyes. We pulled up to the Sanders residence within four minutes.

Mrs. Sanders, around seventy, met us clad in purple gardening gloves and a faded paisley dress. She knelt in the garden repotting some columbine into gaudy orange plastic containers. A cloud of tiny white butterflies scattered when we approached—just another typical scene from the retirees in Wildwood.

"Well, it's about time." She got to her feet to greet us.

"Mrs. Sanders?" I asked. "I'm Sergeant Jim Monday. This is my partner, Bob Cannon."

Bob took it from there. "Mrs. Sanders, we had a report of stolen property. Could you tell us exactly what was taken? It was hard to understand you on the phone."

The lines are often sketchy out here in the sticks.

Bob pulled out his official green notepad and poised his ballpoint pen above the page.

Mrs. Sanders pointed a muddy spade at us. "It's that Wilkes boy across the street. I've known him since he was knee-high to a grasshopper, and I just can't believe it!" Her wispy gray hair waggled back and forth as she shook her head. "No, siree, I just can't believe it!"

"What's that, ma'am?" I prodded. It was always best to keep the witness talking. Even the tiniest clue could help break a case wide open. If we had a thief on the loose, we needed to "nip it in the bud," to quote a famous TV deputy.

She pursed her lips as a monarch butterfly perched on the rim of her oversized 1980s-style glasses. "He's completely changed. I wouldn't have known it was him if I hadn't seen him with my own eyes. He was out in the forest behind my house prancing around as if he was possessed." She narrowed her eyes. "Almost as if he weren't even in control of his actions! Like a marionette."

"A marionette, you say?" Bob jotted the details on his green notepad.

"Yes, a marionette! And he was waving my butterfly net around like a maniac." Mrs. Sanders shook the spade as if it were a conductor's baton. "You know as well as I that these kids nowadays get started on drugs earlier and earlier. Pretty soon they're going to be dancing and jerking around out in the street and get run over."

I reigned the conversation back to the issue at hand. "Is that the stolen property you mentioned? A butterfly net?"

She lowered the weed tool. "Not only that, but he took several of my columbine transplants. I was saving those to give to the Ladies Aid Society members." She pursed her lips. "My reputation as a generous friend is at stake. If I have no columbine to share, I'll get called greedy."

"Yes, ma'am." I held back a roll of my eyes. Heaven forbid someone call her greedy, yet here she was raising cane about a butterfly net she probably hadn't used in over fifty years.

My gaze fell to the row of seven recently repotted columbine plants that lined the yard between us and the victim. Columbine spreads like wildfire and can take over a flower bed quickly. Bob is always telling me of his wife's headaches due to weeding columbine that has squeezed out her zinnias or pansies. You'd think Mrs. Sanders would be happy someone had taken some of those rabid plants off her hands.

Mrs. Sanders shook the spade at me. "I know what you're thinking. 'That old biddie has plenty of columbine to give away. Why is she complaining about a few missing pots?'" She narrowed her eyes. "It's the principal of the matter, Sergeant Monday."

"Yes, ma'am." I nodded at the appropriate pause and waited for her to continue.

"If you let that young man get away with theft, he won't stop there. They never do." She shook her head vehemently.

"Perhaps it isn't the Wilkes boy," Bob suggested with a raise of his forehead. "Maybe word got out that you were giving away columbine, and someone stopped by to take you up on the offer." After all, everyone in Wildwood knew about Mrs. Sanders's eternally-spreading garden.

Another butterfly came to rest on the tip of her spade as she shook her head. "You just check up on that Wilkes boy, and you'll see what I mean. He's going to end up like all the other drug addicts. First, he steals a butterfly net and columbine, and next it will be a car to pay for his habit."

We got the Wilkes boy's address, directly across the street, and headed that way.

"Jim, you think she's right?" Bob said.

I shrugged. "Drugs can get a hold on kids at a young age, but it's best we follow up on all the angles. If Wildwood has a new drug problem, we need to stop it."

The residence turned out to be a home and business in one—the Curl Up and Dye Hair Salon. Mrs. Wilkes answered the door with a pair of scissors and a comb in her left hand.

"Yes? May I help you? Do you have an appointment?"

"No, ma'am. I'm Sergeant Jim Monday from the police department. This is my partner, Bob Cannon. May we come inside?"

She blinked at us. "Of course. Do you mind if I finish up this haircut while we talk? Now that my husband and I are divorced, I need every cent I can earn to keep my son fed."

"Not at all, ma'am," I replied. It's always best to keep potential witnesses calm and relaxed.

She led us through a parlor stacked with fashion magazines to a side room where she went back to work snipping the split ends from an elderly lady's retro 1980s permed short hair. "Now what can I do for you, officers?"

Bob flipped open his green notepad. "It's about your son, Mrs. Wilkes. We've had a report that he stole a butterfly net and several pots of columbine from Mrs. Sanders."

The 1980s short perm took a fatal jagged cut at the back. Mrs. Wilkes steadied her scissors, wiped them clean, and stowed them in her pocket. The customer swiveled herself around in the hairstylist's chair as her eyes flamed with the potential for new gossip.

"But Brandon has always been such a well-behaved child, officer. Usually, he spends all day in front of his video games. I can barely get him to go outside for fresh air." She shook her head. "Do you know yesterday was the first time he went outside and didn't come back until evening?"

Bob scribbled the facts on to his notepad. I suppressed a sigh. The Wilkes boy was definitely involved in some sort of secret. Maybe Mrs. Sanders had been on target with that drug hypothesis.

"I can't think what might have gotten into him." With a sigh, Mrs. Wilkes tossed herself into the second hairstylist's chair, which swiveled her halfway to the wall with a rusty creak.

"Mrs. Sanders seems to think it might be drugs," I stated. "She says she saw him dancing around in the forest with the butterfly net and the pots of columbine as if he were under the influence of some substance."

"Drugs? But Brandon is only eleven. I don't know where he would have gotten them. Aside from yesterday, he's only been here playing video games," Mrs. Wilkes pointed out. Meanwhile, her customer, a veritable gray-haired sponge soaking up gossip, glanced from me to Bob to Mrs. Wilkes.

Bob shook his head. "In our line of work, we see drug addicts that young."

I rushed to clarify. "We're not saying your son is under the influence, ma'am. We're merely required to check out the facts."

The customer ripped away the styling cape around her neck and jumped to her feet. The styling cape, printed with a kaleidoscope of butterflies, sent a powder of gray and white hair snowing through the home salon.

"If you ask me, I think it's Mrs. Sanders who's under the influence," she spouted. "As many medications as she takes, she's probably gotten them all mixed up and is seeing things that aren't there." She shook out the cape, folded it, and reached for her purse. "Here, Melody, let me go ahead and pay you. Keep the change. Same time in two weeks?"

Mrs. Wilkes took the twenty silently and nodded. As soon as the door clicked shut, she rolled her eyes with a groan. "It will be all over town in five minutes. That Myra Stanfield is Wildwood's biggest gossip." She rose to her feet with a shake of her head.

"The boy hasn't been proven guilty," Bob pointed out. "We're just following up on Mrs. Sanders's complaint."

Mrs. Wilkes nodded. "Well, I can't tell you where Brandon is at the moment, but as soon as I see him, I'll talk to him. If he did take those items, I'll need to deal with him now before it becomes a bigger problem."

"Yes, ma'am," I said. If it were my son, I would have been just as worried.

"And to think I was happy when he took a day off from his video games." She shook her head. "Now I have to worry about him ending up as one of your hardened drug-addicted criminals."

I left her my card and asked her to contact us the

moment her son returned home. Bob and I made our way outside toward the patrol car. It was then I noticed the empty plastic bucket rolling in the breeze at the corner of the Wilkes' front yard. I stooped to pick it up—an orange, round plastic planter with traces of potting soil in the bottom.

"Bob, does this look like one of Mrs. Sanders's potting containers?" I asked.

"Sure does, Jim. Doesn't look good for the Wilkes boy, does it?"

"Doesn't look like it."

We took it back to the car as evidence. That's when the next call came in. Mrs. Reeves, Wildwood's 103-year-old citizen, phoned in a complaint. Her butterflies were missing.

"Butterflies?" Bob echoed as I put the car into reverse. "Does she keep them as pets?"

"Who knows? This day is turning into an episode of *Saturday Night Live* by the minute."

Bob merged onto Main Street and locked on to the red light at the end of the path. Mrs. Reeves was always calling to complain about things that most folks wouldn't dream of bothering the police with. Last time, it had been a package of sliced cheese that contained fifteen instead of the standard sixteen slices. She had insisted we arrest the grocery store clerk who sold it to her. "Better check it out, or she won't sleep a wink tonight."

"Neither will we," Bob replied.

He was right. She would keep calling until someone came to check things out. After all, we had been hired to keep the peace.

Mrs. Reeves, behind her century of wrinkles, was clearly distraught. "My butterflies are missing, Sergeant Monday, and I want you to find them. They're always around my columbine. Mrs. Sanders gave them to me last summer because the butterflies love them."

Bob took out his green notepad. "Tell me all about it, Mrs. Reeves." That would keep her happy.

"Well, as you know, butterflies are fascinating creatures..."

Meanwhile, I took a look outside. The patch of columbine was indeed behind the house. I saw no suspicious footsteps, no foul play evidence of butterfly homicide, or a single insect stirring in the garden. The place was practically a graveyard. If there had been butterflies here before, they had left for greener fields.

Greener fields.

I snapped my fingers. That was it.

I returned to Mrs. Reeves's house just as she was handing Bob a homemade chocolate chip cookie. "Bob, let's go. I have a hunch about those missing butterflies."

He flipped his green notepad shut. "Mrs. Reeves, we'll be in touch. Thanks for the cookie. It's just like the kind my mother used to make."

I explained my theory to Bob as I jumped into the driver's seat and squealed into a three-point turn back toward Mrs. Sanders's residence. "Let's check the forest out behind Mrs. Sanders's house. If the Wilkes boy did steal those columbine plants, the butterflies may have left Mrs. Reeves's garden for them. Greener pastures and all, you know."

"And the butterfly net?"

I shrugged. "If he's out to catch butterflies, that would explain the net, wouldn't it? And the columbine would attract them."

Bob nodded. "You're right, Jim. My wife's columbine is always surrounded by butterflies this time of year."

We screeched to a halt outside Mrs. Sanders's house and darted into the forest beyond. She had claimed she'd seen the Wilkes boy here dancing like a marionette. We split up and searched in different directions. Every branch rustling in the breeze set me on edge. There was a good chance we were closing in on the culprit. Any minute now, the case would burst wide open.

A tinkling sound like running water hit my ears. Pushing through a thick blanket of Alabama kudzu, I came upon a clearing. There, next to a stream, was a freshly-planted batch of columbine and a swarm of monarch butterflies intermixed with several smaller white ones—much like the ones from Mrs. Sanders's garden. Just beyond them danced a skinny child in cutoff jean shorts and a *Star Wars* t-shirt. In his right hand, he waved the stolen net as he leapt toward the swarm of butterflies.

The butterflies evaded him as if they had been doing so for millennia, yet he laughed and grinned. His laughter was contagious. I smiled with relief. No drugs involved!

"Brandon Wilkes," I whispered. He matched the description to a T. Just like a butterfly emerging from its cocoon, this young man had experienced a complete metamorphosis from video game addict to nature lover.

I reached for my cell phone and sent Bob a text: *Culprit found. No sign of drugs, but he's heavily under the influence of the beauty of butterflies.* I filmed a quick five-second video and sent it along.

Looks like Mrs. Reeves isn't the only one! Bob texted back.

NOTE: LATER THAT DAY, "TRIAL" was held in the Wilkes's living room. Mrs. Wilkes scolded her son up, down, left, and right for stealing the butterfly net and Mrs. Sanders's columbine. The suspect claimed he wished to watch the fluttering beauties for his own amusement: "They're so graceful!" He was sentenced to community service in Mrs. Sanders's garden and now intends to pursue a career in lepidopterology, the study of butterflies and moths.

(WITH APOLOGIES to the 1960s police show *Dragnet*, which inspired this piece.)

38

A STORM OF BUTTERFLIES

BY VICKI ERWIN

The cloudless blue sky seemed in direct contradiction to the weather forecast I watched while I ate my morning yogurt. The meteorologist said, “Weather Impact Alert” at least thirty-five times, enough that it became meaningless background noise. My butterflies at my Zoo job were much more reliable at forecasting the weather. I’d check with them.

After stacking my dirty dishes in the sink, I grabbed my backpack and locked the apartment door. My two roommates—a necessity to live in a neighborhood close to work—left earlier for their more traditional office jobs. I did not envy them.

Skinker Boulevard was clogged with traffic, so I crossed quickly and carefully, then stepped into Forest Park. A slight breeze ruffled the tree leaves highlighted by sunlight. I glanced at the fountain in the middle of the small lake at the foot of Art Hill, then waved to the statue of St. Louis as I passed. Bikes whizzed around me, going faster than the cars, drivers taking time to enjoy birds, trees, flowers, and nature. All of this was my “office building.”

Before I entered the Insectarium—yes, the house of bugs—my home away from home, I paused to appreciate the Zoo while it was quiet and empty of visitors. *How fortunate am I to be one of the few invertebrate keepers here?*

I stashed my backpack and greeted coworkers in the break room. The conversation, as I expected, centered on the predicted weather.

"Did anyone notice how perfect it is outside this morning?" I reminded them.

"Shannon, you've lived your entire life in Missouri. It can be summer one minute and winter the next," said Chris, who I teasingly called *Spiderman* because of his obsession with arachnids.

I shrugged, trying not to give in to the weather preoccupation.

"Since it's so nice today..." Chris paused and grinned. "Why not have lunch with me by the lake?"

My face heated at the invitation I'd waited for. "Sure, if we don't blow away by then." I giggled, part nerves over the sort-of date, part worry about the increasing clouds and wind. Would something as basic as weather upset this long-awaited chance with Chris? "What do your spiders have to say about it?"

"Nothing so far. At least not to me. Maybe they're talking about it among themselves," Chris said. "What about your butterflies?"

"About to go ask them."

My co-workers gave me some leeway in the way I treated and talked about butterflies in human terms. I liked them much more than some people I knew.

Inside the butterfly dome, butterflies, moths, and dragonflies fluttered through trees, landing for short times here and there. Everything seemed normal. I stood, quietly waiting, for my favorite butterfly to come say hi. Again, my coworkers didn't take me seriously when I claimed Mabel, a marbled white, recognized me. I set the container of her favorite treat of spoiling fruit among the leaves. Finally, she came, circling my head and then alighting momentarily on my shoulder. Her wings whispered as she flew past my ear. I knew it was her because butterflies may look the same, but they have unique markings. Mabel had almost solid white dots along the black mid-wing. Others had varying groups of white dots among the black. My Mabel had been with us for three weeks, and I hoped she'd stay awhile longer, although I was aware butterflies had a short life span.

Once the Zoo opened, my assignment was to make sure none of our flying friends escaped, either fluttering through the open door or hitching a ride on the clothes of a visitor. It would be boring if not for all the guests' questions and comments. And after lunch, I'd move on to a new assignment.

"We came early to beat the weather," said a woman who looked like she was in nominal charge of a group of school age boys.

"But it's so nice outside. Why do we have to be in here?" one of the boys asked.

"Fill out your scavenger hunt card. I think you're looking for a blue butterfly. Your team captain has a camera to take a photo," the woman said, shaking her head as she herded them inside the dome.

"Watch where you step!" I called after them.

When the group returned, the woman approached me. "There don't seem to be as many butterflies today. Does it have anything to do with the coming storm? That might be the interesting fact our team has to bring back to the large group—how butterflies can sense weather."

Visitors referred to everything in the dome as a butterfly, no matter what it was. I peeked inside. It seemed a little quieter. "They do sense changes in the weather—pressure, humidity, wind. But looks like rest time to me." I stubbornly resisted any connection between their behavior and the predicted weather.

"Boys, be sure to include that in your notes. You didn't see as many butterflies as usual because they were taking shelter from the coming storm."

The boys ignored her, smacking each other as they pretended to brush butterflies off their buddies before the teacher herded them out with a look of apology in my direction.

A woman pushed a stroller with a napping baby and pulled a fussing toddler through the chain between the dome and exit. She examined her children for any hitchhikers.

"I think the weather is turning," she said. "It always makes Jessie a fuss budget. And usually when we're here, the butterflies flock around her, but today there were only a few, and they flew right past us."

I couldn't ignore a second report of reduced butterfly activity. I stepped inside, turned in a circle, and looked up. The trees formed a canopy inside the dome, and usually, it was dotted with flying butterflies and moths. There *were* fewer this morning, and the sun seemed to shine less brightly through the plexiglass panels.

Hmm. Mabel had alighted under a tree, and a pile of leaves partially covered her. That was a clear sign bad weather was on the way. I thought the dome might protect the insects from sensing any weather changes, but now I wasn't so sure. Other flying friends had disappeared completely. They were right to hide from rain, but that wouldn't be an issue inside. Outside, even a drop or two on their wings could make them so heavy, they couldn't move and became easy prey. Although there are no predators in the dome, it's an inbred protective mechanism.

"There's a storm raging west of here," Merrilee, my supervisor, said, joining me. "And it seems most of our guests are clearing out."

I moved to the door, and as it opened, a gust of wind blew dust and leaves inside. The blue sky, which had been so bright a few hours ago, had dimmed and turned a dingy gray.

My stomach tightened. Perhaps I should have listened to that weather report. The change in behavior of the butterflies and other flying creatures within the dome belied my rejection of bad weather. I inhaled slowly and let it out. They would be fine inside. I would be fine as well.

"Why don't you take a break, Shannon, and I'll sit here. Although, there doesn't seem to be much need of it, since we have no visitors." Merrilee paced back and forth. She wiped her hands along her khaki shorts repeatedly.

Her nervousness was contagious. A prickle of fear grew inside me, and I, too, wanted to walk it away. I gladly left, grabbed my lunch, and stepped outside, intending to eat by the lake, before the weather worsened.

"Hey, Shannon! I thought we were going to lunch together!" Chris called after me.

"Merrilee wants me to go now." I stood at the door, tapping my toes. The air felt damp and heavy. It added to my growing edginess.

"I'll see if I can get away and join you."

I waited. Outside, it was eerily quiet. The water animals were nowhere in sight. The temperature had dropped, and the wind picked up even more. I turned to go back inside and almost ran into Chris.

"Not a good day for a picnic?" Chris tried to keep his dark hair out of his face as gusts of wind played with it.

My hat kept my hair in place, but I needed to hold on to it to keep it from flying off.

Chris said something else, but the wind carried his words away. Then, a storm siren blared, making it even more difficult to hear what he shouted. I turned back toward the Insectarium, but he grabbed my hand and pulled me in the direction of the main Zoo building.

Pressing his mouth against my ear, he yelled, "It will be safer in there." In the midst of my fear, a tingle of excitement raced along my neck as we ran together.

Leaves, twigs, and even dirt swirled around us as the wind propelled us toward the building that housed classrooms, offices, a cafeteria, and gift shop. Raindrops fell hard as we approached, and the doors slid open automatically. Guards standing on either side directed us to move further away from the doors and windows.

Small children cried, and adults talked in hushed voices. Rain pounded, and the building shuddered as the wind roared. Crashes sounded all around. I dared to look toward the large glass doors and saw a tree splinter and fall, then another.

"This is why the spiders were so active before I left," Chris said. He seemed energized by all the crashing and roaring.

The noise of the wind reverberated in my ears as the crack of trees falling sent waves of fear along my spine, leaving me shaking.

I pressed close to Chris; his arm wrapped around my

shoulders. "Some of my butterflies were taking cover, but not all of them. We should be there."

"Much safer here," Chris said.

"But our bugs." I rarely called them *bugs*, but it was what came out. I had to push the words through quivering lips.

"They're safe. They know when to take cover, and the building is sturdy."

"You said we were safer here!"

"That plexiglass on the dome makes me wonder a little."

And that was where my butterflies and moths and turtles and all the other creatures I cared about so deeply were. I buried my head in Chris's shoulder.

The rage of the storm pressed against my body. The noise was oppressive, roars, crashes, the cries of others who had taken shelter with us. But all I could think about was our animals. Yes, the butterflies, especially Mabel, were first and foremost in my mind. But the bears, the cats, the hoofed animals, the elephants. Hopefully, their keepers had time to move them to shelter—or the beasts themselves knew enough to seek protection.

It could have been a year, or a minute. My sense of time had completely evaporated. But the sounds faded in the distance, leaving only rain, falling more gently, and the creaking of displaced trees as they settled. I moved away from Chris and toward the glass doors.

I gasped. Outside, it looked like a bomb had exploded.

"Ready to go check on Mabel?" Chris asked, taking my hand.

His felt so warm, clutching my cold fingers. I nodded, and we dashed into the rain.

We swerved around trees blocking the paths, and I scanned the spaces around us to make sure no animals had escaped and lurked beneath the fallen branches. Rain soaked through my shirt before we covered the short distance to the Insectarium.

And the damage was worse than I had imagined. Trees had fallen and punched through the plexiglass panels forming the dome. Still, a canopy of leaves remained and covered the interior for the most part. But if any of the winged creatures could find a way, they would escape.

We waited for the door to open automatically. When it didn't, Chris pounded on it. "It's Chris and Shannon! Let us in!"

Merrilee struggled to push the door open enough for us to enter. "Tornado," she said.

Somehow, I'd known it was far worse than a "storm," but how much worse had it been? What else had it destroyed? Was my nearby apartment building still standing? Were my friends and parents all right? My knees weakened for a moment, then I took a deep breath. My first responsibility was to the bugs.

"It's the dome that we need to worry about," Merrilee said. "There's some damage. As soon as maintenance assures us it's safe, we need to check on the insects and animals."

"Are there sections gone?" I asked. "The butterflies and moths—"

"There are, but we've prepared for this exact scenario. As soon as it's safe, we'll gather as many of our flying friends before they escape," Merrilee said as she handed out nets, basket cages, and trash cans.

Chris went to check his spiders, crooning soothing words to them. And he teased me about anthropomorphizing my butterflies!

A maintenance man finally gave us the thumbs up, and we hurried inside the butterfly house, gently gathering the inhabitants with our nets and placing them inside the mesh baskets. *How long could they survive inside a basket? How would we feed them? Could the dome be repaired quickly enough? Or, could we find an alternate home for the time being?*

"The director of the Sachs Butterfly House will be along as soon as possible to transport the flyers to their facility," Merrilee said, answering my unasked question.

"Will he be able to get through? How are the roads?" a co-worker called across the room. "We can ferry them if the streets are clear."

"I'm sure there are roads and streets that are blocked. It depends on where the tornado hit," Merrilee said.

"Did any of you see how many trees are down just here at the Zoo?" I said.

It was like everyone sighed simultaneously at the thought of what we'd lost.

"Anybody hurt? Any animals hurt?" someone else asked. It was hard to see who was speaking through the leaves.

"Not a final report, but so far everyone and every animal is safe," Merrilee said.

After we captured the butterflies and other flyers, there was still cleaning to do. Large chunks of plexiglass rested in the trees and on the paths. Chris helped remove those.

I searched in the capture baskets, in each tree, and under the leaves, everywhere for Mabel. I found her male counterpart, also black and white but with different, more distinct, white markings where Mabel's were blurred, and still no sign of her.

Merrilee sent me to prepare the cocoons and chrysalis for transport to Sachs, the butterfly house in the county. They would keep them in their incubator for now.

Occasionally, thoughts of my family, my roommates, the condition of my apartment would creep in between my concentration on the destruction in front of me. Would the tension that the tornado had left behind in my shoulders and back ever go away? Finding Mabel would go far to easing it.

We worked late. And hard. I wasn't sure I could find the energy to do anything beyond fall asleep on the floor of the Insectarium. And I hadn't seen a flutter of Mabel.

"Where did you park?" Chris asked, once we were dismissed.

"I walked." Would I be able to get through all the fallen trees? We'd heard reports and seen pictures on our phones of the destruction in the park. The rest of the Zoo, however, had survived well. And there were no injuries to staff, animals, or visitors. That wasn't true in the rest of the city, though. There were injuries, perhaps deaths, and miles of destruction.

"I'll drive you," he offered.

"If we can get through," I said, grateful not to have to drag myself the short distance home.

My parents had already checked in. They were fine; in fact, they'd had some wind, no rain, and like now in the park, the sun was shining in Crestwood. Pure Missouri weather.

From news reports, we knew the tornado had traveled north from the park. That meant my apartment was at least on the edge of the storm. Houses we passed on the short drive were missing roofs, windows were broken, and trees were down everywhere. I was almost afraid to see what damage my building had suffered.

Chris parked and insisted on making sure I still had a place to live.

The large oak tree in front of the apartment had fallen across the street. A blessing really. If it had landed any other direction, it would have crushed someone's home. It did, however, block the street. A group had gathered around it, seeming to discuss how to deal with it.

As Chris helped me climb over the tree to get to my front entrance, in the foliage, I looked for random butterflies that may have escaped the Insectarium. Especially Mabel.

At least one of the windows in our apartment was already boarded over. Pieces of roofing were scattered about the yard, and gutters hung loose. My roommate's Mini-Cooper was under the fallen tree, the worst damage so far. The structure looked mostly intact. Other homes and apartments nearby hadn't been so lucky. But directly next door, the building looked the same as it had when I left in the morning. No damage at all.

I lifted my hand to push my hair away from my face. I'd lost my hat long ago. Something tickled my finger. Slowly, I moved my hand level with my eyes. It was Mabel, hovering, almost touching my nose. In my excitement at finding her, it was difficult to remain still. Was she excited to be free or had she found me, looking for safe harbor? As much as I wanted to capture her, I waited. I hoped she would land on my hand. She fluttered away, then back into my line of sight, holding steady for a few moments. Then, she flew off. My heart sank. It was like losing a friend.

As she disappeared, I swallowed my tears—some for my butterfly, some for my community. Mabel was free. She had never experienced that, born in the Insectarium and spending her life under the dome. What a wonderful chance for her. I brushed the few tears that had escaped from my cheeks.

"Was that..."

"Mabel." The tension I'd carried since the storm hit

loosened slightly. I reached out to balance myself on the fallen tree, She was okay. Everything was going to be okay.

A black and white butterfly like Mabel held significance. She symbolized duality. In this situation, I decided it meant destruction and rebirth. Yes, there was destruction all around us, more for some than others. But the city, its people, and me, would be gifted with new life. There were caveats, of course. We would have to work together to make the rebirth happen, and it would take time and money. Together we were strong, and Mabel, strong enough to weather the destruction herself, was a symbol of that.

My coworkers would laugh at me. We were scientists, not romantics. I was both. A duality. The city was as well. St. Louis had encountered and survived worse. Destruction, then rebirth.

Mabel had disappeared. Her remaining days, perhaps weeks, would be spent free.

Chris put his arm around me, and I pulled open the door to my home. I hoped for a last glance of my favorite butterfly, to no avail. I'd have to make do with my favorite Spiderman.

Author's Note

On May 16, 2025, St. Louis was struck with an EF3 tornado. It tore through Forest Park, home of the St. Louis Zoo, destroying the dome of the Butterfly House and taking down as many as 3,000 trees—yes, that number is correct. It continued for over 20 miles, causing five deaths and millions of dollars of property damage. Immediately, citizens of St. Louis rose to the challenge and began the process of clean-up and rebuilding. There is still a lot of work to do.

39

PAINTED LADY

BY JINXIE R. THORNE

Painted lady, Monarch of all beauty.
How can you fly up so high?
Fearless, and free of everything,
Gliding 'cross the clear blue sky.

Beautiful Monarch, you dance on the four winds
The sun, your spotlight, leading your way.
Brilliant orange, dappled black and white.
Precious soul, messenger of light.

New beginnings, we eagerly wait.
Shall we dance with you? Or laugh, or sing?
Painted Lady, you lift our spirits.
Sweet harbinger, what joy do you bring?

40

CODENAME: THE BUTTERFLY

BY BRUCE BUCHANAN

LaKesha Thompson sat on her bed, laptop propped on her legs. The teenager nudged the speaker icon to amplify the news video streaming on the screen.

"...tragedy averted today in Charleston as the Cerulean Blur faced off with Man-Gator after the villain rampaged in the downtown district. The Cerulean Blur, who recently returned after a 17-year absence, risked her own life to..."

A short, gray-haired woman in a brown tracksuit poked her head through the bedroom doorway.

"Time for bed, LaKesha. Tomorrow, you graduate from high school!"

"Will do, Aunt Shirley. Just want to see this story."

A light blue streak zipped across LaKesha's computer screen. *Bet the Cerulean Blur doesn't have any problems when she's running 2,000 miles an hour. Least she's not a freak like me.*

The news story ended, and LaKesha clicked the "X" button. She unfolded her long, thin body, got out of bed, and latched the bathroom door. The teenage girl removed her button-up shirt, leaving on her tank top.

Wings, do your thing.

She flexed her shoulders and two brightly colored wings —purple and blue panels with white borders—popped out from her back.

With a mental trigger, LaKesha's wings gently flapped, lifting her three feet off the hardwood floor. She hovered for several seconds and kicked her bare toes in the air.

The Cerulean Blur is down, and Man-Gator is closing in. I don't think she's going to be able to move... but wait! A new hero has flown in for the save. A hero with wings.

LaKesha fluttered in the narrow bathroom as she relived the scene she had watched on the news. Then one of her wings bumped the door, throwing her off balance. She braced her hand against the sink to keep from falling.

She exhaled deeply. *Some superhero I'd be. Besides, as soon as anyone found out my wings were real, I'd spend my days as a lab rat. Or worse—I'd become a target for some super-villain like The Puritan or that new armored creep, Katalyst.*

After retracting her wings, LaKesha leaned into the adjacent living room. "Goodnight, Aunt Shirley."

The seated woman looked up from her tablet and flashed a wrinkled smile. "Come sit with your auntie for a second." Aunt Shirley patted the burgundy sofa's upholstered cushion.

The century-old floorboards creaked under the tall, skinny teen's bare feet. She sat cross-legged on the couch and Aunt Shirley put a gentle hand on her niece's knee.

"I can't wait to post all my pictures of you on Facebook after tomorrow's ceremony. That'll show all those people who didn't think you'd make it. I knew you would, baby."

LaKesha leaned back on the well-worn couch and sighed deeply. "Big deal. Who doesn't graduate from high school in 2025? And I had to double up on my classes to make it without going to summer school."

Her aunt snorted. "Those other kids didn't go through... you know."

"The 'Big Nap.' No need to sugarcoat it, Aunt Shirley." She leaned over and took a long sip of her aunt's frosty Diet Coke, filled to the brim with crushed ice. "I spent the first six months of senior year in a coma. It is what it is."

And when I woke up, I had these wings.

LaKesha stared out their living room window at Greensboro's Southside neighborhood, on the edge of the city's center. Modern townhomes built in the past five years stood tall like a prodigy child next to humble houses constructed a century prior. Buckling structures under the care of their elderly residents, as if one day they'd bow out entirely to give way to the new. LaKesha and her Aunt Shirley lived in one of the latter homes, a bungalow tucked away on a narrow side street.

"Yes, but you didn't give up." Aunt Shirley squinted at her tablet over the top of her bifocals. "I was looking at the community college's website. You can take your first two years there, then transfer those credits to a four-year school."

LaKesha turned away and propped her chin in her hand. Sports cars zipped up MLK Drive, heading into the city's bustling restaurant and club scene on Elm Street. *People with places to go. Must be nice.*

"I'll give it a look. Right now, I just want to get through tomorrow." LaKesha stood on stork-like legs, hands on bony hips.

"Oh. Okay. Give me a hug then."

LaKesha responded with a quick arm-over-the-shoulder pat, then retreated to her room.

Just want to get through everything.

~

After an uneventful graduation ceremony the next day, LaKesha retreated to her bedroom. She hadn't even changed out of her graduation dress when her phone buzzed.

Anissa. LaKesha narrowed her eyes at the icon on the screen. She and Anissa had been best friends sophomore and junior years. They took the same classes and marched side-by-side in the high school band.

But LaKesha's life got put on hold for six months, after she collapsed while getting ready for school. The doctor's didn't know what to make of it. Her vital signs were normal, but it was like her consciousness... retreated somewhere far away.

Meanwhile, Anissa kept on living. She'd made new friends during the Big Nap. Which is why LaKesha hesitated before touching the icon.

UR going to Grad Night Celebration, right? Plz girl!!

LaKesha's thumbs danced in circles over the glowing screen. Finally, they produced a short reply:

Guess so. See you there.

She set the phone on her bed and dug around in the drawer of her antique chest of drawers. From it, she fished out a bright purple and dark blue Lycra bodysuit with white trim.

At first, LaKesha hadn't planned on attending Grad Night Celebration. *A costume party? Sounds like something rich white kids on a Netflix teen drama would dream up. "Oh, Miss Waldorf? Might I escort you to the costume gala?"*

But then, the idea of going as a superhero hit LaKesha. This was a costume party, and she had always loved superheroes. *No, "loved" isn't the right word. More like "admired." Takes something special to risk your life helping others.*

Initially, she planned to cosplay as an existing superhero —maybe the Cerulean Blur or a gender-swapped version of the Centennial Sentinel. *Heh. Sure shook a lot of folks when "Lady Liberty's Favorite Son" came out.*

But then LaKesha had the idea to create her own costume. She lucked into finding a big pile of stretchy fabric at a Downtown thrift shop. She bought several yards in a variety of colors. Using colored pencils, a sketchpad, and Aunt Shirley's sewing machine, she noodled with a few ideas until a lightbulb flicked to life in her head.

Why not make a costume to match my wings? Not that she intended anyone else to ever see those wings. They were her secret. Her shame. But it could be her private joke.

She held the costume up to her chest. The purple, blue, and white garment flowed down her body—a perfect fit. LaKesha examined the stitching. Every panel came together exactly as it should. A bit of warmth stole its way into her core.

Not bad. But... She threw the costume across her bed, then sat at its edge. Her hands sagged in her lap.

If I go to Grad Night, I'll see a hundred people I know. And they'll all have the same question: "What's next, LaKesha?"

She lay back on the bed and covered her eyes with her hand. Before long, she drifted into a dreamless sleep.

THE SHRILL DRONE of sirens rousted LaKesha from her nap. *Huh... what's that?*

She blinked away stickiness and shook out fog. LaKesha jumped out of bed and opened her window's blinds. An audible gasp sucked all the air from her lungs.

Flames exploded from the high-rise apartment building

straddling the edge of Downtown and Southside. Firefighters' hoses poured water into the blaze. But the fire drank greedily and continued to climb. Thick black smoke flooded the city sky, obscuring LaKesha's view of the inferno.

LaKesha brought her hands together in front of her mouth, as if to pray. *Surely, everyone got out. Because if they didn't...*

She turned her back on the scene blocks away. *What could I do if they didn't escape? I'm a freak. I'm certainly no hero.*

In the dark room, the fire's glow reflected off the mirror over her dresser. LaKesha put her hand on the doorknob. She wouldn't see the fire from their living room. She could lounge on the couch, under Aunt Shirley's crocheted blanket. The morning news would have all the details on the fire, including any victims.

The purple, blue, and white costume called from the closet floor. She lifted it and kneaded its slick fabric in her fingers.

It wouldn't hurt to take a look. I'm not a hero, but maybe I'll see something that can help. Yeah, I can be the eyes in the sky.

She slipped on the snug costume, which fit her like a second skin. Her face grew hot, and she wrapped her arms around her body. LaKesha normally opted for loose-fitting T-shirts and baggy shorts. But after a moment, she stood to her full height, arms at her side. The mask covered her hair and face, but her nose and mouth remained exposed, allowing her to breathe freely.

Wings, do your thing.

Her multi-colored wings popped out from pre-cut slits on her costume. She opened her window, took a deep breath... and jumped.

Before gravity could catch her, LaKesha's wings fluttered. Tiny movements, but powerful enough to push her forward through the hot late spring air. She extended her arms forward, like a swimmer. That helped her cut through the air's resistance.

Getting to the fire by car or foot would be nearly impossible. Police had blocked off streets for blocks surrounding the blaze. But by air, LaKesha covered the distance in less than a minute.

"Hey! Izzat one of those superheroes?" LaKesha didn't look down at the voice below. Her eyes focused on the blazing building. Even a block away, her face warmed from heat pouring off the fire. The air shimmered like a desert mirage. She squinted against the inferno's intensity.

Although the fire was concentrated in the building's lower levels, it was climbing to the upper stories. *No way the firefighters can get through that to help anyone up top. I'll look there.*

With a mental nudge, LaKesha peeled up at a ninety-degree angle. When she reached the top floor, she slowed her wings' pace to circle the building.

"Help! Over here!"

She strained to see through the smoke. Then the movement of waving arms hailed her from a top story balcony.

LaKesha flew close to the building. The heat pressed against her. Sweat beads dripped from her forehead, and she coughed to clear the smoke from her throat.

A young woman and a boy—probably around seven or eight—screamed on the balcony.

I... I hadn't planned on getting involved. But if I don't, they'll die. LaKesha balled her fists. Then she zipped to the balcony.

"Grab hold." She reached out. "I'll take you down."

The woman draped her arms around LaKesha's shoulders, and the young boy grabbed her waist. She hugged both, then flapped her wings. They strained to hoist three bodies, but they slowly lifted the weight off the concrete balcony and carried them over the rail.

Once they were in open air, LaKesha's challenge was slowing their descent. Again, her wings proved up to the task. They took them quickly but safely to the pavement, where she released her grip and allowed EMTs to hustle the woman and her son to safety.

I did it! They were in danger, and I saved them. Like the Cerulean Blur would have.

LaKesha bent over, hands on her knees, to compose herself. The woman she had saved drew deep breaths through an oxygen mask. "Yuh—you need to check on Mr. Yi. He's got a bad leg. And I know he was home tonight."

LaKesha's mouth grew dry, and not just from the smoke she had inhaled. The flames had climbed higher up the building. Fire now consumed the apartment where she had rescued the woman and child. *What if I got lucky the first time? I could die if I go back up there.*

She bit her lower lip. *No. I have to. I'm the only person who can save him.*

LaKesha straightened her back, ran back toward the building, and flexed her wings. But before she could look, a coughing fit seized her lungs. The smoke had grown thicker. *All the more reason to wrap this up.*

She zoomed around the corner. Flames jumped out of the balcony door, blocking any passage into the apartment. LaKesha looked into the bedroom window. Only a thin wooden door separated the bedroom from the fire in the next room.

LaKesha's hand flew to her mouth. An old man lay motionless on the floor. *Is he...?*

No. Mr. Yi tried to rise up with his arms. But he slumped back to the floor.

A weight dropped into LaKesha's stomach. Either she would save him, or he would die. Maybe they both would.

LaKesha flew away from the building—far enough to breathe in some clean-ish air. She spun and launched herself toward Mr. Yi's window at full speed. Her shoes slammed into the glass, sending a crystal spray across the bedroom.

"Mr. Yi!"

Cough, cough. He looked up at LaKesha and extended his hand.

She picked up the frail old man with relative ease and held him in her arms. "Let's get you out of here, you and me."

CRASH! Before she could fly them back out the window, a wooden beam tumbled through the fire-weakened ceiling. The dangling hunk of burning wood separated them from their escape route.

Her heart racing, LaKesha backed away. The far wall stopped her progress. Nowhere else to go. LaKesha's breathing raced, and not only from the lack of clean air.

They were trapped.

She couldn't get past the flaming beam hanging down from the ceiling. Certainly not with Mr. Yi in her arms.

LaKesha put her hand against the door. Even through gloves, the heat nearly burned her palm. It wouldn't be long before the fire in the living room consumed the presswood door. Perspiration poured down her face and stung her eyes.

C'mon, girl. There's got to be a way out! What would the Cerulean Blur do?

Then, a glimmer of the day's remaining sunlight caught

her eye. She looked up. When the beam fell, it ripped a hole in the roof. Not big enough to fly through, but only a layer of plywood and some shingles surrounded the tear.

It wasn't much of an escape route. But LaKesha had to take it.

"Hang on, Mr. Yi. The flight is about to get bumpy."

LaKesha cradled the old man to her chest and launched herself at the ceiling, pushing her wings to their maximum ability.

Got to time this just right. As she flew, she cocked her right fist behind her ear, then brought it forward to meet what was left of the burning roof.

She put everything she had into that punch. When she smashed through the roof, sparks exploded like Fourth of July fireworks. They burst forth into the evening sky and kept climbing.

LaKesha opened her mouth and inhaled deeply. Who knew muggy, smoky air could taste so good? She and Mr. Yi were fifty feet above the burning, but now empty, building. From up here, she could see for miles in all directions. A wave of euphoria made her whole body tremble, so she wrapped her hands tightly around the man's waist to ensure she kept her grip.

I could get used to this view.

The EMTs had an ambulance waiting for Mr. Yi when she returned to the street. One of them said, "He's swallowed a lot of smoke. But his vitals look good. I think he'll make it."

Another rescue worker handed LaKesha a water bottle, which she gulped down. But as she prepared to fly away, a middle-aged firefighter in a red "CHIEF" helmet waved to her.

LaKesha took another deep breath. "Look, I'm getting

out of your way. If this is the part where you tell me not to meddle in fire department business, I get it."

"No, you don't get it at all!" Tears smeared the soot staining the man's lined face. "Before you came, some of my people and I were going in to save those folks trapped on the top floor. And... we weren't all coming out."

He put a shaking hand on LaKesha's shoulder. "Not only did you save three lives up there, you saved a bunch down here. Mine included, probably. I don't know how to thank you, young lady."

LaKesha turned away. Her lip quivered. "You don't have to." With that, she soared into the darkening evening sky.

A moment later, LaKesha found a perch atop one of Greensboro's few office towers. The apartment building still burned, but not as fiercely as before. The firefighters' efforts had kept the blaze from spreading. And no one had died, thanks to LaKesha.

She propped her hands on the rooftop guardrail and leaned forward. A huge smile crossed her face.

What's next? I'm not exactly sure. But I know it involves helping people. Because that Big Nap? It wasn't a setback. It was a rebirth—a chrysalis. And I'm not a freak or a loser or a lost soul.

Who am I then? You can call me... The Butterfly.

41

A MULTITUDE

BY VICTORIA L. SCOTT

"Welcome, daughter Calliope," the AI door chime chirped in a sing-song voice.

The apartment door slid open. I took a deep breath, as if that would prepare me for what I had to do today. I clenched my fists hard, then released them, shaking them out. No matter what happened, I couldn't let Mom see how heavy-hearted I was.

"Mom? It's time."

She looked up from the datapad, where random numbers and words filled the screen. The bland-faced servo-nurse stood by, monitoring her charge as Mom filled her days with tasks vital to her, but nonsensical to everyone else. I wondered, bleakly, if this was going to be a good or a bad day.

"Oh! Callie." She ran a shaking hand through her short grey hair. "My goodness, it's been so long since I've seen you."

"I was here yesterday, Mom," I said gently. I came every day.

As an archaeologist, I was an expert at finding and carefully removing delicate artifacts from the ruins of long-lost civilizations. My daily visits with Mom reminded me of the process of articulating something from the dirt. It took careful brush strokes, removing soil in increments, to reveal a fragile pot or a long dead skeleton. In her case, each day I visited, I saw another incremental loss of her memories and grasp of the world around her. It was the inverse of what I did to retrieve an artifact. The disease's progression brushed away who she was with small strokes, but the cumulative effect only revealed the hole that removal left behind. Knowing what she'd been like before, it was hard to accept how much she'd lost over the past three years.

My mother, Dr. Arsinoë Anastopoulon, had been a marvel once. When I was a child, she'd been the smartest person I'd ever known. She encouraged me to pursue my passions with the same enthusiasm she did her own, cheering my successes and wrapping me in hugs as I found my own calling. Now, her mind slid into an endless, pointless activity she could neither explain nor stop. The doctors could do nothing but watch as I did. As we all did.

"Time?" she asked.

I cleared my throat. "Ah... You signed up to help with the terraforming project. I'm taking you to the research office one last time."

Mom tilted her head. "Terra-forming? Didn't I work on a terra-forming project?"

It surprised me that she remembered her career. Something within my mind unclenched a little. *Today may be a good day.* "Yes, Mom. You headed the project a few years ago."

That was before the dementia spun her mind away from evaluating soil readings and plotting atmospheric changes. When she found a way to link biological patterns to synthetic organisms to speed up the terraforming process, it changed worlds. Once she perfected her technique, what initially took centuries shortened to a decade. Planets became habitable overnight when measured on a galactic scale, all because of her. She didn't remember the awards, or the cities named after her on the three moons of Jupiter she'd helped to make habitable.

Hearing in news feeds about her former colleagues continuing her work was a two-edged sword for me, with pride at her accomplishments buffered by despair, knowing she was not that person anymore.

She put the datapad down precariously on a pile of random books. With a purposeful expression on her lined face, she stood up and stepped carefully toward me.

The servo-nurse floated over to keep the data pad from falling to the floor, ready to spring into action if Mom was unsteady on her feet. I moved in to take Mom by the hand. She met my eyes, and for a moment, she was 'Dr. Arsi,' planetary transformation expert. The brief flash of understanding I saw reminded me of happier days.

"I'm helping with plant propagation," she said, patting my hand.

I dropped my gaze. "Yes. Ah... Dr. Ngum says they're ready for you."

She smiled. "Isn't that good news? Why are you sad?"

"I'll miss you, Mom," I said, my voice breaking. My determination to honor Mom's final wish was the only thing keeping me moving forward.

Mom squeezed my hand. "I'll miss you too, but I'll be flying. Won't that be wonderful?"

I tucked her hand in the crook of my arm, and we headed for the door. "Yes, Mom," was all I could say. I put an arm around her as she shuffled out of the apartment, wondering if she truly understood she was leaving it, and ultimately me, forever.

~

Mom marveled at the shuttles moving around us as the autopilot took us to the building on the Moon where her office had been. Before the disease crippled her mind, Mom told me she found the grey, lifeless expanse of the lunar landscape outside her windows as a personal challenge.

Her brow lowered as she looked at the Moon's surface while the autopilot steered us into the airlock.

"There aren't any plants," she said, looking back at me. "How can I fly here?"

There was a muffled clang and the hissing sound of air pressurizing in the corridor on the other side of the hatch.

"You'll be working on a different planet, Mom," I said, unbuckling her seatbelt and helping her to her feet. "Here is where they send you to the planet where you'll fly."

The hatch opened. We stepped into the airlock, then into the corridor beyond, where all her terra-forming colleagues stood, smiling and welcoming. They were putting on a brave face, something I was finding harder to do. I looked up and blinked several times to keep the welling tears from rolling down my face.

Mom gripped my arm tightly. "Who are these people?"

Even though her lack of recognition should not have come as a surprise, it felt like a punch to the gut. My voice hitched as I said, "You used to work with them. They've not seen you for a long time, and they've missed you."

Her grip loosened. "Oh," she said to me, and then, beaming at the assembled people, waved and said, "I'm here to learn how to fly."

The others waved back, troubled, looking at each other in dismay. They'd known the disease meant she wasn't herself, but they hadn't lived with it as I had, helping her remember words and how to do daily activities.

When she headed the project, Mom knew everyone she worked with well. She'd filled her office with holograms of colleagues' families celebrating children's birthdays and significant life events.

I doubted she remembered any of their names now.

Dr. Ngum, now the head of the terraforming project, stepped forward, all politeness. He stood a foot taller than Mom, his dark skin a stark contrast to his white lab uniform. His smile was forced and sad.

"Dr. Arsi, how good to see you," He said. He met my eyes for a moment. "I'm glad your daughter, Calliope, came with you. Was it a pleasant trip?"

"I think so," she said, looking to me for verification.

I nodded, smiled for Mom's benefit, and indicated she should add more to her answer.

Taking her cue from me, she beamed and said, "It was."

Dr. Ngum held out his arm. Mom took it without hesitation.

"Let's get you settled," he said, leading us to the bio-chamber interface.

GETTING Mom ready for the biometric transfer took ten minutes. She smiled as the tech applied the cap with the sensors to her head and tested everything to be sure the computer accessed her thoughts. Her patience amazed me. I wondered if she truly understood what the wires and equipment did as dread filled my heart. The nightmare of what her life had become was almost over.

Dr. Ngum directed her attention to a monitor with an image of thousands of chrysalides in a large rectangular clear-sided case, each with a sensor attached to it. Beyond the case, I saw the red dirt of Mars, dotted with flowering plants.

My stomach clenched. Mom wanted this, I told myself.

"Dr. Arsi, are you ready?"

She nodded, her expression thoughtful. Then she reached out to me, taking my hand.

"Thank you for letting me fly," she said.

A sob escaped me as I kissed her hand. "Oh, Mom, you're welcome. I love you," I said, and nodded to Dr. Ngum to begin the procedure.

When the biometric interface program scanned healthy minds, the subjects had a headache for a day or two but suffered no other ill effects. Once she found out about her diagnosis, she knew what the procedure would do to her damaged brain. She'd wanted 'one last chance to change a world,' and after she signed the consent forms, we both wept.

There was no sound as the computer destroyed what remained of my mother's mind, feeding her chaotic thoughts to the chrysalides. It surprised me that, in that moment I felt proud, since it was so like her to make her last act one that brought life to another place. What was it like, I wondered, to awaken on another planet in a new form? Would she have any memory of her life with me? Would she be sad to leave me behind?

That had been one part of her terra-forming innovation, after all, using human mental patterns to increase the efficiency of genetically altered plant propagation insects, like butterflies. Used *en masse*, the insects into which the computer programmed my mother's crippled mind would spread across the surface of the red planet, visiting flowers and pollinating everywhere they went.

I watched the monitor. The chrysalides pulsed with life, opening to reveal butterflies with wings in a riot of colors unseen on Earth.

As Mom's head sagged onto my shoulder, the butterflies lifted off in an exuberant cloud, fluttering away to fulfill their mission and make Mars habitable for humanity.

I let out a cry, finally able to express the sadness and despair I'd held captive for so long. I'd kept my promise, and now she was gone forever. I clutched her shoulder and howled at the unfairness of her final years as the disease brushed away the woman I'd known with tiny, devastating strokes.

The technicians left then, respectfully, leaving me to my anger and grief.

I held Mom's lifeless body close, sobbing as I watched her fly, a multitude on a planet 140 million miles away.

42

CHRYSALIS ROCK

BY PAUL GOAT ALLEN

Chrysalis • (noun) a quiescent insect pupa, especially of a butterfly or moth: ***the transformation from egg to caterpillar to chrysalis and, finally, adult.***

The old man who lived at the end of the long, winding dead-end road—the one with the "No Trespassing" sign chained on the wooden gate—understood many things. He knew he was dying. He also knew he had wasted away the entirety of his life—almost 70 years gone with nothing to show for it except for aching bitterness and regret that twisted like voracious tapeworms in his soul.

And he was certain the world was reaching its end. Like him, the planet was tired, sickly, failing. What was once a thriving wilderness outside his front door was now an eerily silent wasteland. The countless tree frogs and their hypnotic nocturnal songs during the warm months were long silent. No buzzing bees flittered from wildflower to wildflower in the morning light. The songbirds were gone. No deer breakfasted on sweet grass in the meadow. The old man hadn't seen a butterfly in years. Plants of all kinds struggled to grow and ended up stunted and misshapen. It was as if all the color and vibrancy were slowly being leeched from the natural world, leaving only a sad reality existing in muted sepia tones.

Hidden away inside his dilapidated shack of a home, curled up in his bed under a cocoon of moth-eaten blankets, the old man waited for the world—or his frail beating heart—to give up the ghost. Existing in a never-ending semi-conscious state somewhere between dream and nightmare, he obsessed about the transgressions of his past: all the pain he had unnecessarily inflicted on people, all of the lives negatively impacted by his cruelty and willful ignorance, all of the beauty and joyful moments in his life he so callously ignored. A loving wife, now free from the misery-inducing union and happily remarried. Three adult children, all estranged and hundreds of miles away. No friends. Not one person who even cared if he lived or died.

But as the days dragged into weeks, and the weeks into months, the old man didn't wither away. He buried himself deeper under his chrysalis of dirty blankets and listened as the earth entered a long sleep, dreaming a planetary dream of perpetual grayness and mind-numbing cold. A never-ending gloaming stretching across the world.

Hidden away on a remote tract of land, the old man's house was forgotten by time and as seasons passed in the frigid twilight, the house fell to ruins piece by piece. First the front porch, already rotten, crumbled; then parts of the roof caved in; and, one by one, the windows cracked and shattered. Pipes burst. Mold-covered drywall collapsed in on itself. Metal nails turned to rusty dust. But still, curled in his chrysalis, the old man somehow survived, tormented by his dreams of guilt and remorse.

Eventually, the house and everything in it disintegrated around the old man in his makeshift cocoon, leaving only a small mountain of dirty blankets open to the elements. Seasons of freezing rain, snow, and mud turned the old man and his blanket fortress into something resembling a massive stone.

Deep inside the chrysalis rock, the old man began an unlikely transformation...

CHRYSALIS • **(noun) the hard outer case enclosing a chrysalis:** ***the splitting of the chrysalis and the slow unfolding of the wings.***

THE OLD MAN didn't know how long he had been in his Kafkaesque limbo—months, years, centuries?—but he eventually realized that something had changed.

He had changed.

Self-loathing and regret were replaced by strange new feelings: contentment and acceptance. The old man was intimately aware of his failings, his deepest character flaws, and all of his misguided decisions in life. But these shortcomings made him uniquely who he was and he not only embraced the imperfections but sensed an opportunity to learn from those mistakes and become something... more.

The soul-numbing cold that had been an ever-present companion for as long as he could remember slowly, almost imperceptibly, withdrew—like a massive ice jam breaking up one chunk at a time and drifting downstream. Instinctively, he felt the urge to stretch, to push at the tight confines of his blanket boundaries. Eventually one of the blankets weakened and a small tear appeared. With it came the faintest ray of light...

CHRYSALIS • (noun) a transitional state: *she emerged from the chrysalis of self-conscious adolescence.*

UPON EXITING HIS CHRYSALIS ROCK, the old man knew many things in an instant. Although he was acutely aware his corporeal body was still seemingly the same—he could see the dark liver stains marking the crepe-paper skin on his hands—he knew he was fundamentally changed. Transformed. He felt lighter, unencumbered, free. He also knew that the world hadn't died as he thought. It had blanketed itself in its own massive protective shell and slept through a vast darkness in order to be reborn—it had become a planetary chrysalis rock orbiting the sun.

The old man, still weak from eons of inactivity, crawled to a nearby stony outcropping, sat down, and took in his surroundings. A lush, rolling valley spread out before him. Swarms of golden bees buzzed nearby among a kaleidoscopic ocean of wildflowers. The smell, an intoxicating floral perfume that reminded the old man of honeysuckle, was almost overwhelming. A massive indigo butterfly with luminescent white spots that resembled constellations on a celestial sphere sailed by like a supernatural sign. A new world. A new chance to live, to exist, to become. A chorus of songbirds sang out in the distance, the whistles and chirps creating a melodious soundtrack to the old man's new life.

Understanding the miraculous transformation he had somehow experienced—the opportunity to be reborn, to experience life again, even if only for a day or a week or a month—brought the old man close to tears. Instead, he gloried in the sunlight warming his skin, the breeze whispering across his face, a furry caterpillar crawling across his big toe. And although he hadn't emerged from his chrysalis with wings, his spirit soared up into the sky.

A mother hare with its babies startled when the old man's laughter rolled through the meadow like joyous thunder.

A new day had begun.

AUTHOR BIOS

A. L. Paolucci is a romantic fantasy writer and poet. Her work often contains messages of mental health and learning to take care of our minds and spirits. Whenever she isn't writing, she's usually drawing or painting in her studio.

A. N. Griffith, an author in the Appalachian Mountains, draws from her lived experiences to craft stories featuring resilient heroines who find family, live with chronic pain/disability, grieve, and will not be defined by their circumstances. She hopes her stories will make others feel welcomed, wanted, and seen.

Abigail Davis spends most of her free time escaping reality through the realm of books. She is an enthusiastic participant in her local poetry and writer's groups. Her work is found in One Page Poetry's 2023 Anthology, her local poetry zine *Poetic Voices*, and the blog *Writing in a Woman's Voice*.

Adele Liles has been a high school English teacher for 26 years. She has two contemporary YA novels with Wild Ink Publishing and has work published in several anthologies. She lives with her husband in Virginia, where she can be found writing, reading, or watching a ridiculous amount of reality television.

Alana Avellino is a poet and storyteller from Ontario, Canada. Her debut poetry collection, *Deary Diary* (2025), explores resilience, identity, and self-belief. Through her work, including her poem "Becoming" with Wild Ink Publishing, she hopes to remind readers they are never alone in their journey of healing and transformation.

Amanda Dodge is an author of magical realism and speculative fiction represented by Najla Mamou at Savvy Literary Services. For the past seven years, Amanda has worked as a full-time ghostwriter based in Michigan. Outside of writing Amanda is the proud mother of a high-needs autistic boy.

Bri Eberhart is a speculative fiction writer who lives near Buffalo, NY, with her husband and two cats. She is the author of Strangers in Our Heads and Strangers in Our Hearts. Her stories have also been published in multiple online magazines. You can find her on Twitter & Instagram.

Bruce Buchanan is the author of *The Return of the Cerulean Blur* (May 2026, Wild Ink Publishing), the redemption story of a former superhero. His first book, the New Adult fantasy novel *The Blacksmith's Boy* was published in 2025, and the sequel, *The Queen's Daughter*, is coming in December 2026, both from Wild Ink. Bruce lives in Greensboro, N.C.

Casie Bazay is the author of the YA novel, *Not Our Summer,* and various works of short fiction. She lives with her family on a hay farm in Oklahoma and enjoys reading, dancing, caring for her many, many animals, and exploring the great outdoors at every opportunity.

Chaylee McCleese is a partner teacher at a charter school where she teaches small ELA groups. She uses her platform and writing to advocate for patients with autoimmune conditions since she has psoriatic arthritis. Her debut Young Adult Novel, *Pitiful Peaches* will be published in the spring of 2026.

Cody Draco is an emerging queer poet, settled but never stagnant, creatively restless in the rural sanctuary of southern Kentucky, United States. Unflinching yet deeply human, his poetry pushes boundaries while distilling meaning from the void of 21st-century existence in an intentional effort to code a new masculinity.

Dana Gricken is a multi-genre author from Ottawa, Canada, published by Melange Books, Evernight Teen, Oliver-Heber Books, and Bella Books, as well as different anthologies. In 2019, she was given a writing scholarship by actor and director Kevin Smith and wants to write 100 novels in her lifetime.

Desirae Gracyn is a nurse and neurodiverse slash queer writer. Working with patients, she has seen how powerful words are in healing and escaping, and it revived her childhood dream of being an author. She predominantly writes fantasy and hopes to help others escape in the worlds she creates.

Dr. Lester N. Linsangan is a teacher at Nueva Ecija University of Science and Technology, an internationally published author, and a literary mentor. He guides students and professionals in writing and publishing. With a deep passion for literature and education, he is pursuing his Doctor of Philosophy in English Language and Literature at La Consolacion University Philippines.

E. H. Perry is a Middle School Latin teacher and author. In her free time she loves to read and craft. She is forever grateful to her wonderful husband who helps make time for her to write, and her amazing daughter who is starting to write stories of her own.

Erin Jo Eldry is a Central Florida author, dabbling in both poetry and adult fiction. Selections of her work have appeared in various literary anthologies, and her debut novel, *A River Like Mine*, is slated for release in July 2026.

Geneviève Laprise is a chronically ill, neurodivergent, French Canadian author with over 25 short-form publications in venues such as Cold Open Stories, Knee Brace Press, and Wishbone Words. She enjoys spending time outside and at museums with her family. She would love to someday open a bookstore café.

Geraldine Ann Marshall has a degree in zoology from the University of Kentucky. She has had books, both fiction and nonfiction, as well as poems, stories, and articles in journals and anthologies, published in the United States, Europe, and Australia. A mother and grandmother, Geraldine lives with a dachshund-beagle.

Heather J. Hassig lives in Richmond, Virginia with her husband and two young children. Formerly an English teacher, she now teaches preschool by day and works on her second novel by night. She loves traveling, reading, and sharing her children's joy in the small things.

Holly Goode is enjoying living life with her husband, son, and small zoo of animals. She loves falling into rom-coms and romantasies that leave her swooning for more. When not writing, you can find her working as a nurse educator, fostering kittens, and winning all the best board games.

Jinxie R. Thorne has always enjoyed reading, and creative writing. She is a loving wife to her husband of ten years, and caring Pet Parent to her furbaby "Baby Fluff".

Kay Deborah Linley is a northern interdisciplinary

artist who weaves together themes of healing and nature in her writing, paintings and fibre arts. She released her first book, *Paddling Back to Us*, in 2022 and is working on a poetry book about teachings and healings from the natural world.

Kelly Grabovac is an engineer by day and a historical fantasy author by night. She focuses on history's forgotten heroines, and loves to write about Slavic, Greek, and Roman mythology. When she's not working or writing, she's traveling the world with her husband.

Kendra Ann Keplinger, a graduate of Seton Hill University's Writing Popular Fiction program, resides in her home among the hills in West Virginia, pouring her heart into stories as both a teacher and author. She dedicates this to her family, fiancé, friends, teachers, and work family, including her students.

Kristen Argyres is a wife, mom, and author. Though her preferred genre is fantasy, she also writes for charity anthologies to flex her writing skills. *My Thorns For Your Roses*, Kristen's retelling of the Scottish faerie tale "Tam Lin," debuts with Conquest Publishing April 14th, 2026.

Laura Jordan is a thriller and horror author represented by Carleen Geisler at P.S. Literary Agency. She's been a finalist for Authored's 2024 Rising Talent Competition and Wicked Whispers Competition as well as shortlisted for the 2025 and 2023 RevPit Competitions. She also experiences aphantasia as depicted in her **Kaleidoscopic Quill** piece.

Lianne Robinson writes stories steeped in faith, family, and the feeling of home. Her debut, *The Messiah Project,* releases in 2026, with *Holiday Connection* to follow. A wife, mom, and aspiring chef, she has contributed to several anthologies and loves gathering folks around a table filled with food and laughter.

Lindsay Schraad Keeling is the author of *The Funeral*

Director's Wife, a dark romantic thriller that was published in 2024 through Conquest Publishing. It was a finalist for the Best Thrillers Awards, and all proceeds are donated to Oklahoma Homicide Survivors Support Group. She received her MFA in Creative Writing from Southern New Hampshire University in 2022, and has been part of several anthologies as well. She resides in Virginia with her husband and fur babies.

Michelle Sanchez is the author of young adult Gothic horror and dark fantasy inspired by classic literature and atmospheric settings. She's represented by Rena Rossner at Deborah Harris Literary and is equally obsessed with reading, writing, and coffee. Follow sanchez_m_m on Twitter/X if you'd like to connect.

Mickey Black is a writer and poet from Richmond, Virginia. She has appeared in several anthologies, including *The Greatest Holiday Romance Stories Ever Written* by KissMet Quarterly, and *Tread Lightly, Speak Gently* by Wild Ink Publishing. Be on the lookout for her debut romance novel, *When Mountains Crumble*, releasing in 2026.

Having channeled her life-long obsession with stories into writing, **Morgan Matlow** has a Bachelor's of Arts degree in Creative Writing. In her free time, she can be found concocting new recipes, traveling the world, or exploring the mountains near her home in Northern Utah with her husband and dog.

Natalie Nee is a novelist and latte enthusiast. Her work has appeared or is forthcoming in Across the Margin (Best of Across The Margin, 2023), Rejection Letters, Pithead Chapel, Maudlin House, Cowboy Jamboree Press, BULL, Tiny Wren Lit, The Hooghly Review, and more. She's cooler on Twitter (@novelnatalie).

Nathaniel Mendoza is a writer from the Philippines.

Currently pursuing a Bachelor of Secondary Education at Nueva Ecija University of Science and Technology, Nathaniel is passionate about language, literature, and education. Their work focuses on love, melancholy, and life's reality. When not writing, they are listening to music and reading books.

As a genre fiction book critic, **Paul Goat Allen** has written more than 10,000 reviews for companies like *Publishers Weekly*, *Kirkus*, the *Chicago Tribune*, and BN.com. He has published stories in a wide variety of categories, from crime fiction to romance to folkloric fantasy. He is also an adjunct instructor and mentor in Seton Hill University's Writing Popular Fiction graduate writing program.

Pines Callahan is a former geriatric psych nurse turned professional native plant nerd. When she's not wrangling a wild 5th grader, she's at the beach or in her garden. She has short stories available through Wordfire Press, From Beyond Press, and Wild Ink Publishing.

Rebecca Linam loves researching details and discovering unique settings and twists to use in her writing. She also writes short stories for magazines and literary journals and has written a series of Open Educational Resource textbooks for students of the German language. When not writing, she enjoys sewing historical costumes, traveling through Germany, figure skating, and playing the harpsichord. Follow her on Twitter (X) @rebecca_linam.

Rebecca Minelga is an author and speaker who uses the power of words to navigate the liminal spaces between who we are and who we are becoming. When not writing, she can be found open water swimming in her local lake or traveling the world on an adventure!

Riley Klabunde is a multi-genre writer with an MFA

and MA in creative writing. Her work spans fantasy, romance, and speculative fiction, rooted in character, emotion, and rich worldbuilding. She also runs Compass Point Creative, supporting authors and small businesses, and divides her time between Scotland and the United States.

Russell Chamberlain was born in Nashville, Tennessee, but currently lives in the Pacific Northwest with his family. He writes short stories, fiction, and poetry. He had three nonfiction pieces published this past winter and spring, one with Waxing and Waning and Beyond Words Anthology, and another with Alternate Route.

Sally Lotz is a four-time published children's author, short story writer, and book coach. She lives in Florida, where she enjoys the beach, browsing through bookstores, writing in coffee shops, or caring for her plant babies. When not writing, she can usually be found listening to true-crime podcasts.

Trinity Pierce is a writer from the PNW. Besides scribbling down stories, she enjoys playing video games and drinking an excessive amount of tea.

Vicki Erwin is the author of over 30 books, middle grade, adult, fiction, and nonfiction. She had no idea she could write short stories until she tried and succeeded while earning an MFA in Writing Popular Fiction from Seton Hill University, proving you can teach an old dog new tricks.

Victoria Scott writes Speculative Fiction. She's had short stories published in *Dragons of a Different Tale*, *Tales of Monstrosity*, and *Cerasus Magazine*. She owns a suit of Roman armor and wears it to the grocery store. She teaches History/Latin and earned her MFA at Seton Hill University.

AFTERWORD

My dearest butterflies,
Oh, how time has flown!

Together we soared to new heights, and found a renewed strength in our life on the ground. We came together, found ourselves, and more importantly, shared our stories with the world. That's what it's all about, and I want to thank each and every author for contributing to this special anthology.

When Demi reached out and asked me to do this with her, it was a no brainer. She is a special friend and such an enthusiastic advocate in this community who is constantly giving to others, and it was about time the community gave back to her. She is the butterfly queen, and I am incredibly lucky to have flown by her side to work on this anthology with her and the team at Wild Ink.

My favorite part about this project was not only seeing, but *feeling* the impact of these stories. From heartbreaking stories of grief, to the hopeful imaginations of a brighter world, every single author brought their own perspective of the theme to the page and it has been so heartwarming to see. To help put your words together, to build a collection of stories and poems that bring a little goodness back into the world, is something I will never be able to replicate and for that, I thank you all.

Demi's idea for this anthology took off as quickly as a butterfly flutters its wings for the first time. From the submission call to making such tough decisions with Demi when reviewing these pieces, to sharing good news and ultimately our publication day, this anthology has truly been a myriad of colors and experiences.

We are all butterflies living in this world, and no matter how dark or hard it may get, it's up to us to let our color, let our passion and empathy flow unto others and make this planet a better place for everyone who walks it. As you can see, everyone has a different perspective or idea of what a butterfly means to them. To me, a butterfly is a symbol of hope. Of kindness and light and pure goodness. Something so small, so delicate, so intricate you can't help but stop whatever you are doing in your busy day to simply admire. It's a reminder to pause, to breathe, to remember the small things and make the most out of your day, out of this one life we get. It's science and love and beauty all wrapped together in a complex design—a kaleidoscopic reminder of humanity.

I encourage you, dear reader, to think about what the butterfly means to you. Is it a symbol of belief, of hope, of rebirth? Does it purely bring joy and kindness to a world that can't possibly receive enough? Whatever you may think, whatever you may feel, I ask that you never let that go. Never get busy enough, never get tired enough, to stop and smell the roses. To stop and watch the butterflies flutter in the wind, moving to their next destination. To admire the beauty in the world, before you leave it.

Like the stories shared in this book, we are all a myriad of emotions and purpose—we are a kaleidoscopic quill, and it is up to each and every one of us how we will write our story. While it's time for this chapter to close, there is always another page to turn, another flower to bloom, another caterpillar to transform.

May your metamorphosis be all consuming.

With love and hope from your Editor,
Andie Smith

www.ingramcontent.com/pod-product-compliance
Lightning Source LLC
LaVergne TN
LVHW091036080826
845145LV00002B/520

* 9 7 8 1 9 6 4 8 8 5 5 7 5 *